JUST ONE SNOWBOUND NIGHT

DEBORAH COOKE

DEBORAH A. COOKE

Just One Snowbound Night
By Deborah Cooke

This book was previously published as **Snowbound**.

Cover by Elizabeth Mackey

❀ Created with Vellum

FLATIRON FIVE TATTOO

Flatiron Five Fitness has a new tattoo shop—run by the enigmatic and legendary tattoo artist Chynna. When the moon is full, Chynna creates one tattoo to set two hearts afire and gives it away, with the goal of making romantic dreams come true. Who will be next?

1. Just One Snowbound Night
(Olivia and Spencer)

2. Just One Vacation Night
(Reyna and Kade)

3. Just One Unforgettable Night
(Lexi and Gabe)

4. Just One Christmas Night
(Chynna and Trevor)

∾

DEAR READER

In the middle of my contemporary romance series, **Flatiron Five Fitness**, Kyle has the idea of adding a tattoo shop to the services available in the lobby of the fitness club. He has the perfect artist in mind—the legendary Chynna, who has recently sold her shop, Imagination Ink. He thinks he can tempt her to open a new venue at Flatiron Five Fitness, and if you've read any of those books, you know that Kyle can be pretty persuasive. He even convinced me.

As much as I love writing a series set in Manhattan, I wanted to mix things up a bit with a small town setting. The small town would be very very small, small enough that three friends would take a girls' weekend elsewhere when they wanted to have some fun. Meet the three friends from Honey Hill, Maine: Lexi, the outgoing party girl (who has a secret), Reyna, the flamboyant entrepreneur (who has a hidden past), and Olivia, the research scientist, who is finishing grad school and the reason for their celebratory weekend in New York.

Olivia has always been hot for Lexi's brother, Spencer, but she's never even admitted it to Lexi. On this particular weekend in New York City, the three friends not only attend the opening of Chynna's new tattoo shop at Flatiron Five Fitness, but Olivia wins a free tattoo from Chynna. The tattoo in question is supposed to bring romantic good fortune to the recipient—when Olivia makes a wish, it's for Spencer. When Lexi learns the truth, she's determined to make Olivia's dream of a night with Spencer come true, before Olivia leaves Maine, maybe for good. Of course, Lexi doesn't play by anyone's rules...which gives Spencer more than a night to convince Olivia to give them a chance.

I love this story of two people acting on their existing attraction and finding that it's so much deeper. I love that Spencer seduces Olivia with his cooking, and I love that she finds a sensory side she didn't know she possessed. I love the fictional Honey Hill, Maine, and hope that you enjoy it too. This series, *Flatiron Five Tattoo*, is complete with four books: one for each of the three friends and one for Chynna, too. There's an excerpt at the end of this book for **Just One Vacation Night**, which is Reyna's story. All four books are also available in print editions.

The *Flatiron Five Fitness* series and the *Flatiron Five Tattoo* series take place in real time. You can find a **timeline** for the series on my website, along with a **list of characters**. They're all under the **Flatiron Five Fitness** tab. I also have Pinterest boards for both series: here's the one for *Flatiron Five Fitness* and here's the one for *Flatiron Five Tattoo*.

You can keep up to date with my contemporary romances by subscribing to my **Heroes & Happy Endings** newsletter.

Until next time, I hope you have plenty of good books to read.

All my best,
Deborah
http://deborahcooke.com

JUST ONE SNOWBOUND NIGHT

PROLOGUE

New York—Saturday, March 31, 2018

Flatiron Five was rocking, just the way Hunter liked it. The music was loud, the DJ was smoking, the dance floor was packed with writhing, bopping, beautiful bodies. He could see the gleam of Kyle's blond hair on the other side of the club—it didn't hurt that Kyle was tall and buff enough to stand out from the crowd. Hunter wasn't a partner like Kyle, but he was glad to be a part of the club he loved more than any other place in the world. The two guys exchanged satisfied nods across the dance floor and they simultaneously gave each other a thumb's up.

On this night, Kyle had his satisfied smile and Hunter knew why. Tonight was to be the big reveal of the new shop in the lobby.

At the stroke of eleven, Kyle raised his hand and the music fell silent, as arranged. He stepped forward to a cheer. "Thank you for coming to the first full moon party at F5!" Kyle said and there was a roar of approval from the crowd. "Are you having fun?" They shouted agreement and stamped their feet. "Only that much fun?" he asked, apparently surprised, and they bellowed agreement again. Hunter grinned, enjoying Kyle's touch with crowds.

"You've made this night awesome and the party's just started," Kyle said. There was another cheer in response to that, but Kyle lifted a finger. "But I had to stop the dancing for a surprise."

"Free memberships!" suggested someone on the dance floor.

Kyle laughed. "You've got it!" he joked then snapped his fingers. Two of the waitresses flung fistfuls of gift cards into the throng. Each one gave the bearer a week of access to the club to try it out and they'd always been an excellent way to cultivate membership. There was a scramble to claim the cards, then shouts as they were held up triumphantly.

"Woo hoo!" Kyle cried. "Welcome to another crop of new members at F5!" He was answered by a cheer and applause. Hunter saw people bouncing, obviously wanting the music to start again. "This last surprise is the touch that will make F5 even more special. Are you ready?"

The crowd cheered, then quieted as the lights dimmed. There were still excited whispers and a hum of anticipation. Kyle gestured toward the door to the club. A trio of spotlights swirled across the walls and ceiling, then focused on a woman who stood alone in the doorway.

When had she appeared? She hadn't been there, and then she had. Hunter wasn't the only one startled by her sudden appearance. She could have been conjured by magic. In fact, she was wreathed in swirling white and appeared to step out of a mist.

She had short hair that was bleached white and tipped in pink. She was dressed mostly in black. Her eyes were outlined with dark kohl and her lips were vivid pink. There was a massive gem at the collar of her flowing white shirt and her black skirt swirled around her ankles. She wore black boots with stiletto heels and a long black jacket with silver embroidery. It looked Edwardian. A frock coat. Her face was pale and achingly beautiful.

Timeless.

The crowd stared.

Hunter stared. He'd seen this artist in the new shop in the lobby, but she didn't look nearly so dramatic in the daytime.

"Chynna," someone whispered with awe and the woman's lips curved slightly.

In one hand, she gripped a silver briefcase. She lifted the other hand and the rings on her fingers sparkled. The crowd gasped as a black bird flew from behind her, appearing just as suddenly out of nowhere, and landed on her finger. She lifted her hand so it easily could step onto her shoulder.

It was a large black raven. It cawed then bobbed its head, seeming to survey the crowd with approval. Its eyes gleamed and Hunter saw that there was something silver on its leg. The woman murmured to it and the bird nodded again.

"'She walks in beauty like the night,'" Kyle said and the woman laughed. Hers was a throaty chuckle that made Hunter think of nights spent in bed, and maybe long afternoons there, too.

Chynna lifted her head to look at him and he had the sudden urge to hide, as if she could see his secrets even from across the crowded room.

Kyle obviously had no similar doubts. He walked toward the woman, joining her in the doorway as he spoke. Hunter thought they looked like moonlight and sunlight together. He glanced toward Kyle's partner,

Lauren, but she smiled as her gaze followed Kyle, her confidence in his intentions complete. "'Of cloudless climes and starry skies; And all that's best of dark and bright; Meet in her aspect and her eyes: Thus mellow'd to that tender light; Which heaven to gaudy day denies.'"

"Lord Byron," the woman said, her words almost a purr of pleasure. She reached out to put a fingertip on Kyle's chest and for a moment, Hunter thought he could see Kyle's tattoo. His chest piece seemed to glow through his black T-shirt, as if it had been lit by fire. Hunter thought he saw the heart tattoo burn radiant for a moment, and Lauren's name blazed, which was impossible. By the time he'd blinked, Kyle's shirt looked normal and Hunter wondered if his imagination was messing with him.

"The moon is full," Chynna said. "There is magic to be worked."

"Please welcome Chynna," Kyle said. A gasp of delight filled the club, and her name was repeated again and again. "The world's most amazing tattoo artist, the one whose work has the power to set hearts afire."

The repetition of her name became a chant. *Chynna, Chynna...*

She bowed to the crowd. "Tonight the moon is full," she said, her rich voice carrying over the crowd easily. "The power of love magic is strong. Tonight, to celebrate my new shop within F5, I will give a tattoo to one of you, a tattoo with the ability to make your romantic desire come true."

There was a ripple of excitement, and Hunter felt that anticipation rise as they jostled forward. A free tattoo from a famous artist wasn't a small thing, whether it was magic or not.

"Me!" cried one woman, then the shouts became

more numerous. Hunter could see that this artist didn't just have a strong presence—she had a reputation and her popularity intersected perfectly with the people who had come to the club.

Kyle had made another perfect choice.

Chynna held up a hand for silence. "But the choice is already made. Tristan will show us." The raven flapped its wings. The spotlights swirled as the bird took flight. Hunter thought it might be dazzled by the lights but it seemed untroubled by them. It flew over the crowd, circling three times, then descended to land with precision on the shoulder of a pretty woman.

She was small and curvy with long chestnut hair pulled up in a ponytail. She looked a bit bookish to Hunter and not like their usual clients. She gasped in surprise but the taller woman beside her laughed with delight.

"Liv! Total score!" the friend cried and gave her a high five.

A third woman, a blond one with a lot of tattoos, tackled Liv from the other side and hugged her tightly. "You're the luckiest person in the world!"

Liv didn't look convinced of that.

The raven cried out as the women embraced and bounced. Hunter could see that Liv was wary. Her friends appeared to be a lot more outgoing, one tall and one curvy, both with some ink. They hooked their arms through Liv's, leading her toward Chynna as if they thought she might not go otherwise.

They might be right. Liv didn't look like the kind of person to get a tattoo.

The crowd parted before them and the bird flew overhead, returning to his mistress.

While the raven had been choosing Liv, Chynna had removed a deck of cards from her pocket. The silver briefcase was at her feet and she fanned out the cards in her hands. Even from a distance, Theo could see that they were over-sized with pictures on them.

Tarot cards.

She lifted them so that only the backs of the cards were visible to the crowd, then held them out to Liv. Liv's friends gave her a push when she hesitated, and she picked a card, turning it to look at it.

"Who is he?" her tall friend demanded and the crowd laughed.

"The object of desire." Chynna plucked the card from Liv's fingers and slid it into her right pocket. She offered the fanned cards to the bird, which was perched on her shoulder again. He cawed and bobbed his head, as if debating his selection, then tugged one out of alignment with his beak. "The mechanism of desire." Chynna added it to her pocket without showing it to anyone. She then chose a third card herself and put it into her pocket. "The end result of desire," she purred. The raven nodded as Chynna smiled. The rest of the deck disappeared into her left pocket.

She touched Liv's cheek with a fingertip. "As you wish, so shall it be," she said, then picked up her briefcase and spun to leave. Her coat tails and skirt flared out as she pivoted. Her heels clicked on the stone floor as she led the way to the new shop. Liv and her friends followed, their excitement clear.

Hunter and more than a few others followed from the club.

Once in the lobby, the raven took flight again and flew over Chynna toward the new shop. Again, it flew three circuits, then dove toward the shop. The bird was the first one over the threshold, and landed on a gold perch there.

Secret Heart Ink it was called, the name filling the

back wall with a red pulsing lit heart at the end of it. The black floor had the phases of the moon in white on it, and there were a lot of black glass tiles that sparkled like they were filled with stars. There were red hearts scattered in key locations. One wall was filled with framed photographs of Chynna's work and there were a lot of fairy lights. A pair of women were standing ready. They were dressed in black, but not quite as flamboyantly as Chynna. One had short black hair and one had long hair that looked like flowing flame.

Chynna ushered the three women into the shop, took another bow, then her employees pulled deep red velvet drapes across the glass walls that faced into the F5 lobby. They tugged the drapes until only Chynna stood framed in the gap. Hunter realized there were hearts embroidered across the drapes.

"Some magic must be done unobserved and by moonlight," Chynna said, her voice coming from everywhere and nowhere. Hunter suppressed a shiver, but the guests didn't seem to share his reaction. They hooted and cheered as the drapes closed, then the music started again and Kyle pointed back to the club.

"Let's dance!" he shouted and they were only too happy to follow his instruction. In a heartbeat, Hunter was alone in the lobby with Kyle and Lauren. Kyle seized Lauren's hand and came to Hunter's side. "So? What do you think?" he asked, that familiar triumphant sparkle in his eyes.

"I liked the show," Hunter admitted as another of the partners, Theo, joined them.

"Another triumph," Theo said, giving Kyle a fist bump. "Looks like a great fit."

"And quite the reveal," Lauren teased. "But then, you're the best tease."

"We all have to stick with what we do best," Kyle replied with a grin.

"Did Chynna do your tattoo?" Hunter asked, indicating Kyle's chest.

"No. She gave me a referral to an artist in San Francisco." He smiled down at Lauren. "I knew that any magical spells would be unwelcome."

"You're persuasive enough on your own," Lauren said, but she didn't seem to have an issue with that.

"Come on upstairs to one of the suites and I'll remind you just how persuasive I can be," Kyle threatened.

Lauren laughed easily. "You just want to make sure I don't change my mind before we get married."

"You'd better believe it."

"Have you picked a day?" Theo asked.

"Still waiting on Lauren's divorce," Kyle said with a grimace. "On the upside, it gives me more time to convince her to get married again."

"It'll be a casual affair when it happens—" Lauren began.

"*When* not *if?*" Kyle teased her and she gave him a little push.

"On the beach in Santa Cruz. Fish tacos all around," Lauren continued. "I want everyone to come, so we'll have to pick a date that works for everyone."

Hunter wasn't expecting that, but Lauren gave him a smile. "You're part of the team, now, too, Hunter."

"Thanks."

"I'll be there," Theo said. "The world needs photographic evidence that Kyle Stuyvesant is a one-woman man."

Kyle and Lauren laughed together, so obviously happy that Hunter smiled. Kyle snapped his fingers then and turned to Theo. "Hey, I should warn you.

Chynna took one look at you and said you get a tattoo free anytime. She wanted to do it tonight, but I convinced her to choose someone from the crowd instead."

"I don't really want a tattoo," Theo said, apparently unable to keep himself from taking a step backward. Hunter was intrigued. Theo was usually so composed. Did he dislike the idea of ink so much as that?

"Or is it magic you don't want?" Lauren asked, her tone teasing.

"Or is it love?" Hunter dared to say.

Theo didn't smile though. In fact, he looked ready to run.

Kyle was studying the other partner, his expression serious. "You know, Theo doesn't share any of his secrets. Never has, now that I think about it. He's worse than Damon in that, but so subtle that it's slipped under my radar." He had a determined look, as if he meant to change that.

"Maybe Chynna has already guessed his secret," Lauren said.

"Well, that tattoo will have to wait," Theo said. He spoke quickly, as if he wanted to redirect the conversation. He wasn't as gracious as he usually was, which intrigued Hunter. Did Theo have a secret love? "I'm heading back west tomorrow."

"Sooner or later, she'll catch you," Kyle taunted.

Theo laughed but it sounded strained. "Maybe, maybe not." He changed the subject with less than his usual grace. "Maybe we could do something similar at F5 West."

They all nodded agreement.

"It's a perfect service to offer this crowd," Lauren said. "And the giveaway is a great idea."

"She's going to do it every month," Kyle said. "She

says it's part of the cycle to give back. I say it's going to be an awesome partnership for both of us."

"I'll see if I can find any good candidates this week," Theo said. "Now, go and remind Lauren why she loves you. Hunter and I will watch the party for the rest of the night. If I don't see you in the morning, try to stay out of trouble."

"You got it," Kyle said and the partners embraced. "Thanks for stacking the crowd. It wouldn't be such an awesome party tonight without your connections."

"Or your instincts," Theo acknowledged. "I'm already thinking about F5's third location."

"Whoa! Let's get F5 West open first!" Kyle said.

"Now you sound like Ty," Hunter teased and they all laughed.

Lauren gave Theo a kiss on the cheek, then walked to the elevators with Kyle, the pair of them holding hands. Hunter and Theo watched as they walked to the elevators, holding hands, happiness coming off them in waves.

"Perfect match, huh?" Hunter said lightly, wondering at Theo's serious mood. "Doesn't everybody want some of that?"

"Not me," Theo said with a finality that surprised Hunter. He winked. "You've got to know your own limitations."

Before Hunter could ask—because he thought the F5 partners could do pretty much anything—Theo headed back to the party, leaving him alone in the lobby. He had a couple of minutes to wonder about Theo's big secret, then he heard a favorite song starting and knew he needed to dance.

～

SECRET HEART INK.

Liv's heart was going to explode. It was still racing, beating faster than ever, and she knew why. She didn't do risk or experiments or even girls' weekends in the city. This was a good reason why. She couldn't believe the raven had picked her, out of all those people. She never won anything. She was never chosen for anything. She didn't like being the center of attention and usually managed to avoid it.

But the bird *had* chosen her. She'd always admired Reyna's tattoos but would never have volunteered to get one herself. It seemed like something a more flamboyant person would do.

Like Chynna.

The stuff about the moon's magic and finding true love was nonsense, of course. Liv didn't believe in either magic or love, but she knew it would be rude to voice her doubts.

Lexi, of course, was loving it all. Comparing their reactions, anyone would have thought that Lexi had won the grand prize. She was practically bouncing in her anticipation and her eyes were shining. She went straight to the sample books and began to flip through them. Reyna was surveying the tattoo shop, her eyes wide with wonder like a kid in a candy store. She was the one who'd suggested they come here, as Chynna had done most of her tattoos.

"This is an awesome place," she said to Chynna. "You totally scored."

"I love it," the artist confessed.

Lexi was turning the pages of one of Chynna's portfolios. "What are you going to get? I saw your face, you know. Who *is* he?" she demanded again. "And why haven't you told me anything?"

"Liv and her secrets," Reyna teased, her eyes

sparkling. "I knew we'd get to the bottom of at least one this weekend."

"Big adventure in the city," Lexi said.

"Or tequila," Reyna replied. "Whichever works."

"Liv never drinks enough tequila to lose control," Lexi complained. "Good thing the raven had your number."

Liv didn't answer her. She loved her best friends to bits, but she didn't have anything like their verve.

Stepping out of her comfort zone had to end badly.

It invariably did.

"Maybe Lexi should get the tattoo," she said when the curtains were drawn. "Or Reyna. She has lots already." There were just the six women in the shop, but Liv didn't feel as if she had much in common with any of them.

Chynna gave her an amused glance. "Tristan didn't choose Lexi or Reyna. He chose *you*." She had set her silver briefcase on a table and opened it now, revealing the collection of tattoo guns packed inside. Each one was in a special compartment, carved out of the dark foam lining to fit it perfectly. Liv guessed that they were customized, because Reyna leaned closer for a better look. Chynna caressed them, her fingers sliding over each one lovingly.

"Why did he choose me?"

"Because he knows who needs the magic most. It's his gift."

Liv bit her tongue. She leaned over the portfolio beside Lexi. What would she get?

"Why is he named Tristan?" she asked to stall for time. Maybe if she asked enough questions, Chynna would toss her out.

But the question didn't seem to annoy her. She

slanted a glance at Liv. "Do you know the story of Tristan and Iseult?"

Liv shook her head.

Reyna cleared her throat. "Weren't they the first star-crossed lovers, the ones some say provided the inspiration for *Romeo and Juliet*?"

"Exactly."

That didn't explain the bird's name, but Chynna didn't say any more.

"Is your real name Iseult, then?" Liv asked and the artist laughed.

She still didn't reply, though. She took the three tarot cards out of her pocket instead and went to the counter by the entry to the shop. More fortune telling, too. Liv kept from rolling her eyes.

"You're skeptical," Chynna said quietly, no accusation in her tone. She laid down the first card, the one Liv had chosen.

The Knight of Wands.

"A man," Reyna explained. "And since it was right-side up, he's arriving in her life."

"Galloping in on a white charger maybe," Lexi said.

Liv felt shivery. Pieces of paper couldn't know anything about her life. Divination was a trick, a game of the odds. She was in her early thirties. Statistics suggested that she was probably heterosexual and she wore no rings. Chynna had made a deduction and probably used some sleight of hand to encourage Liv to choose the card.

It had to have a logical explanation.

"The object of your affection," Chynna said, giving the card a little stroke. "Or perhaps, more accurately, the focus of your passion and lust."

Liv didn't scoff.

"Who knew Liv had passion or lust?" Reyna teased.

"There was a reason they called you the Ice Queen in high school."

"And she hasn't thawed yet," Lexi said.

"Maybe it'll just take the right man," Reyna said. They both looked at Liv, their manners expectant.

"Everyone has passion and lust," she said, knowing she sounded a little stiff. "It's the biological mechanism that encourages us to breed, which ensures the survival of the species."

"It's a lot more fun than that, Liv," Reyna said.

"Maybe you need to do it with Mr. Right to really enjoy it," Lexi said.

Liv could have argued that there was no such thing as a Mr. Right, but she was thinking of Lexi's older brother Spencer. He was so different from her. That's why he'd always fascinated her.

What if she had a one-nighter with him before she left for England?

Too bad she didn't have the nerve to seduce him or even suggest intimacy with him.

"Look at that blush," Lexi said, gripping Liv's shoulder. "Who *is* he?"

She *was* leaving in three weeks. If she made a move now, even if it went badly, even if Spencer did find out it was her, he might forget by the time they saw each other again.

Or, alternatively, she might not ever come back to Honey Hill.

That was do-able.

She liked the idea of seducing Spencer before she left.

Although it might take more than one taste to satisfy this particular biological urge.

"What's the next card?" Reyna asked.

"Tristan's pick?" Chynna asked, then turned over

the second card. It was The Moon. "The Moon governs impulse and urges. It demands that you run wild and follow your primal urges." Her dark eyes sparkled. "The Moon insists that you surrender to your instincts." She slid her finger to the first card and tapped it. "With him."

Liv might not survive any interval of surrendering to her impulses with Spencer.

He'd probably never look at her the same way.

And actually, that might not be a bad thing. Anything had to be better than him treating her like another sister when all she wanted to do was lick him from head to toe, jump his bones, lock him in her bedroom, and have her way with him over and over again.

She was getting wet just thinking about it.

Chynna watched her and smiled.

"A night of wild sex with her fantasy lover," Reyna concluded with satisfaction, cutting right to the chase, as always. She nodded. "It'll be good for her to lose her inhibitions and go for it for once. Come on, Ice Queen, schedule a spring thaw!"

"What do we do to help make it happen?" Lexi asked.

Of course, Lexi saw herself as part of the solution. She was always ready to step up for her friends.

Could Lexi and Reyna help?

"Accept the tattoo," Chynna said, raising her gaze to meet Liv's. "And set your heart afire."

"I'll get you a shooter from the bar if you need encouragement," Lexi offered.

Liv shook her head, her decision made. She hoped she didn't regret it. "No. I want to do this sober." She took a deep breath. "Could I have a tattoo of a bee?"

"A bumble bee? Of course." Chynna shed her frock coat and one of the assistants swooped in to claim it and hang it up. She rolled up her sleeves with care. "Why a bee?"

"Because that's the focus of my research. Genetics in bees and how—or if—it influences them falling prey to viruses and parasites. It's possible that there's a genetic reason why some hives are experiencing large losses of population and others aren't."

Chynna nodded and Liv realized she was moving into lecture mode. She smiled and fell silent as Chynna showed her a few images.

"I'd like one in flight, so it's obviously alive, maybe with a flower."

The raven crowed as if approving of that, and Chynna smiled even as she took a pad of paper and sketched. She was obviously talented, because her pencil moved with confidence.

"No bees sliced up for the microscope?" Reyna asked, making a face.

"I see enough of those," Liv said. "I want to look at the tattoo and think of how they buzz on a summer's day."

Reyna smiled. "In the gardens at The Pines."

Liv nodded. She and Reyna had spent a day at the big house in Honey Hill the previous summer. Liv had watched the bees while Reyna helped Jane with the honey harvest there. She used their honey in the cupcakes she sold, and she sold the honey for the Watkins, too.

It was a bit spooky how Chynna drew exactly what Liv wanted.

As if she had looked right into her imagination and plucked out the image. That was irrational. She must have just described it well. It was bigger than Liv might have hoped, a good four inches across, but she wasn't going to pick nits. This was a once in a lifetime experience and she would enjoy it.

She'd never get another tattoo.

She hoped it didn't hurt too much.

Chynna drew a red heart in the middle of the bee, the only spot of color on the drawing. "That's where the magic goes," she said softly.

"What's the third card?" Lexi asked.

"That's a secret, for now," Chynna said. "It's the result of what we conjure here tonight. You'll find out soon enough, but the card is probably the only way that I'll know. I like to know the end before I participate." She lifted her gaze and gave Liv a smile. "You should tell Lexi and Reyna who he is, since you might need their help."

Liv nodded, bracing herself for Lexi's reaction. "It's Spencer."

Reyna swore softly, her astonishment complete.

There was a moment during which the only sound was that of Chynna drawing.

"My *brother*?" Lexi demanded.

"I don't know anybody else named Spencer."

Lexi blinked, her astonishment clear. "Since when?"

Liv felt her cheeks heating but didn't answer.

Lexi swore. Reyna laughed. "Spring is in the air," she said with a laugh.

Lexi shoved her hand through her hair, paced the width of the shop then came back to eye Liv. "Seriously? Spencer? *Seriously*?"

"Seriously. Why is that hard to believe?"

"He is so hot," Reyna said with a wise nod at Lexi. "You'd think so, too, if he wasn't your brother."

Lexi turned to Liv. "What can we do to help?"

"I don't want him to know it's me," Liv said.

"A secret lover," Reyna mused. "Oh, this will be fun."

"I'll get Gabriel to help," Lexi said, referring to Spencer's partner at Wolfe Lodge. "He'll be up to help with that."

"It has to be a secret," Liv insisted. "One time with no repercussions."

Reyna shook her head, her skepticism showing.

"Don't waste the magic of the new moon," Chynna said, her voice dreamy.

"That's two weeks away," Reyna said.

"We can work with that," Lexi said, purpose in her tone.

The deadline made no sense to Liv, at least not because of the moon. Moons didn't have magic whether they were full or new. But she was leaving for England in less than three weeks and leaving it that long meant that there would be less time for Spencer to find out the truth before she was gone forever.

Liv felt her blood run hot and then cold. Could she really do this?

She had to do it.

She had to *know*.

CHAPTER ONE

Portland, Maine—Sunday, April 15

The plan was nuts.

It was also Lexi's idea, which pretty much explained everything. Liv would never have concocted such a scheme, but that also meant she would never have done anything about seducing Spencer. The plan should ensure that he never knew it was her.

That was the important thing.

Would he play along?

Liv had major jitters but she wasn't going to back down now. She really didn't want to see Spencer be surprised by the news of her attraction to him. She wanted her fantasy but not any awkwardness. Now that her tattoo was healed and the plan was in motion, the only thing left to do was hope for success.

Blindfold. Sex. Getaway.

She had this.

It was new and different, but she'd think of it as an experiment. A test of her verve. A means of getting the desire for one gorgeous man out of her system.

Liv gripped the steering wheel. Would Spencer figure it out?

She was leaving for the UK the next night. She wouldn't be back until the fall. If this went badly, she didn't have to go back to the town of Honey Hill, Maine at all. Ever. Her mom was good with visiting her wherever she ended up.

But the plan was good. It would work.

Liv lowered the window and got a ticket for the parking garage.

There were clouds gathering overhead when she parked at the airport and headed for the terminal. The wind was up and she wondered whether it would rain or snow. Whatever kind of precipitation fell, she'd be back here in twenty-four hours, waiting for her flight to Heathrow.

Liv called Lexi. "I'm not sure I can do it," she said when her oldest friend answered.

"Of course you can," Lexi replied with her usual confidence. "It'll be easy. We'll take care of the tough bit."

"He'll think he's been tricked."

"He'll think he's in heaven."

"I'm going to puke," Liv confessed.

"Don't!" Lexi replied. "It'll ruin everything. Trust me: it's hard to seduce a guy when you've got yack on your coat."

Liv heard Gabriel chuckle in the background. "And you know this because you've tried it?"

"I'm going out on a limb," Lexi admitted. "I'm guessing."

Gabriel murmured something and Lexi laughed. "Okay. There was that incident at a Christmas party a few years back, but I didn't really want him anyway."

"I thought you wanted all the guys at least once," Liv heard Gabriel tease.

"Everyone but you," Lexi retorted. "You're too much of a bad boy even for me."

Liv rolled her eyes, doubting that was even possible.

There was a hoot, indicating that Gabriel had taken exception, and Liv would have bet good money that Lexi had taken Gabriel home at least once. She entered the terminal and checked the arrivals board. "You didn't tell me what you had to do to convince Gabriel to go along with this."

"And I'm not going to. Just trust me."

Liv smiled. Got it in one. "Okay, I'm walking to the gate."

"Good. You remember everything?"

"Yes, diabolical one."

"And everything's ready here. Look out, Spencer! The new moon has your name and number!"

"Does your brother know you should come with a warning label?"

"Probably." Lexi was dismissive.

"Besides," Reyna contributed suddenly. Liv hadn't realized she was there, then wondered where else she would have been. "There will be *cupcakes*."

Liv didn't share Reyna's conviction that cupcakes fixed everything, but she knew that kind of commentary would be unwelcome. "Thanks," she said, because Reyna's cupcakes were awesome. She wasn't sure there'd be time for food. "I hope Lexi has a story to explain Reyna's cupcakes in Spencer's house."

"I'll think of something," Lexi said. "Better yet, smear them around, eat them, and destroy the evidence before he can see it."

Something else to do. Liv nodded, forgetting that Lexi couldn't see her. "Okay."

"Gabriel's going to call him now," Lexi said. "Get ready."

Liv reached the gate where Spencer's flight was arriving. The glass doors were tinted, but the sign displayed his flight number.

He was probably just on the other side, waiting for his bag, maybe fifty feet away.

And just in a couple of hours, he'd be at her mercy. She gripped her phone tighter.

"I *am* going to puke," she said.

"Use it," Lexi said, showing her typical lack of mercy. "If he thinks you've been inconvenienced, too, you'll start with something in common."

"Got it." Liv ended the call and dropped her phone into her purse. She jammed her hands into her pockets and balled them into fists, reminding herself to stay calm. She was the queen of composure. She was impassive. She could do this. Her heart was skipping and her stomach was jittery, but Spencer didn't need to know that. It seemed like her new tattoo was heating up, like she could feel Chynna's tattoo gun burning its outline all over again.

But that was irrational.

As irrational as moon magic.

And true love lasting forevermore.

The doors slid open and three passengers emerged. Strangers.

Liv took a steadying breath.

The doors slid open again, and half a dozen passengers stepped into the terminal. Some were clearly expecting to be met, because they surveyed the crowd. Others trudged away to taxis or to the parking garage.

Six more.

Eight more.

What if Spencer had missed the flight? What if he'd guessed his sister's plan or somehow sensed trouble and canceled his flight? What if he didn't turn up at all? Liv wasn't one to worry but her imagination was churning out possibilities when the doors opened and the man himself strode into the terminal.

Spencer Wolfe, live and in person.

Liv's heart stopped cold, skipped, then raced. He was on his phone, so she had a chance to ogle him.

She hadn't seen him for a while, but he was still as gorgeous as ever. Dark hair, a little long, and a little tousled. He was wearing a leather jacket and jeans, a hoodie under the jacket. He frowned as he talked into his phone. His lips tightened before he said something curt, then he glanced up, his gaze sweeping over the crowd.

Their gazes locked.

Her tattoo exploded in fire and Liv almost fell over at the sudden burst of heat. Was she going crazy? Or was this just stress? The sensation faded as abruptly as it had come on and she could dismiss it. She waved at Spencer and tried to look cool and composed.

It had to be better than looking like she was going to hurl.

She knew Spencer's eyes were a sapphire blue with long dark lashes. She knew they had to be snapping with annoyance. She knew which tattoos he had where, that he worked out daily, that he was an amazing chef, that he was part owner of a successful restaurant and bar, that he seldom drank alcohol, that he had a wicked left hook and a killer smile. She could hear the rumble of his voice as he told Gabriel off, but could only stare back at him, her heart thumping as he strode directly toward her.

Perfection made flesh.

The only man she'd ever wanted.

It was just raw biology. He was the best male specimen she'd ever seen. That was all. Natural selection.

Survival of the species. May the best genes win. Plain old biology getting things done.

It was too late to back out. This was going down. She was going to do it.

And as Liv watched Spencer approach her, she had to admit that she was really, *really* excited.

~

THIS WASN'T LIKE GABRIEL.

Which was saying something.

"What do you mean, you have a date?" Spencer demanded. "You had a date already. You were supposed to pick me up."

"Sorry," his partner said, not sounding very contrite at all. "This is important."

"Well, I think getting a ride home from the airport is important. What am I supposed to do now? Get a cab? Rent a car? It's hours from here to Honey Hill!"

"Olivia said she'd give you a ride," Gabriel said, interrupting Spencer smoothly.

"Olivia? How did she get dragged into this?"

"It was Lexi's idea."

That didn't do anything to soothe Spencer's temper. "That's hardly fair, Gabriel."

"On the contrary, once she knew the situation, she offered. She was driving up from Harvard today anyhow."

"Just because Olivia's nice doesn't mean you're not an asshole."

Gabriel laughed. "God, I hope not."

Spencer scanned the crowd in the arrival area and spotted Olivia, as pristine and perfectly groomed as ever. There was a reason they'd called her the Ice Queen in high school: most of the time, Olivia didn't seem to have any emotions at all. Still, it really pissed Spencer off how his sister used her friend, who was too nice to give back as good as she got. Reyna, at least, put her foot down and said no to Lexi. Olivia never did.

She gave him a cool little smile and waved her fingertips at him.

As if she'd rather be anywhere else in the world.

Sometimes, it bit the wall to be treated like a brother. Spencer would love to make Olivia smile, using means that she would probably find shocking. He'd always wondered about shattering that frost that seemed to surround her, about breaking her free, warming her up, introducing her to pleasure that would make her moan. In fact, he'd love to shock her, to hear her come, to feel her come when she was locked around him.

Oh yeah. He'd fantasized about Olivia for years, but that wasn't going anywhere. She seemed so virginal that he felt like a jerk for even having fantasies about her. He hoped she'd had sex, but doubted she'd ever shouted out loud, awakened the neighbors, or come back for another round. The idea of her being desperate for sex, being hungry for more, demanding what she wanted, was the source of many satisfactory dreams. It was probably wrong that he wanted to be the one to introduce her to such pleasures.

She wasn't interested.

"It's not funny, Gabriel," he said sternly. "You're taking advantage of Olivia."

"Not as much as you think," his partner said, a strange undertone to his words.

Spencer frowned. "What are you talking about?"

"Never mind."

"Wait a minute. How am I going to get my truck back from you? I'll be just as stranded at my place once Olivia drops me off."

"Hey, gotta go!"

Spencer stopped cold, knowing evasion when he heard it. "Did you wreck my truck?"

"A dent. A small one." Gabriel was talking fast, never a good sign. "Should be fixed by tomorrow. Or Tuesday. Wednesday latest."

This was why Gabriel hadn't wanted to be alone in the truck with Spencer for hours.

"Gabriel! I trusted you!"

"Big mistake, my friend."

"You've been talking to Lexi too much," Spencer accused, but Gabriel broke the connection. Spencer stared at the phone unhappily. His truck was damaged. It couldn't be a small dent, not if Cameron hadn't been able to fix it by the time he got home. And now his only way home was with Olivia, who had to have a hundred things she'd rather be doing than driving him around on a Sunday night.

Spencer shoved his phone into his pocket and sought Olivia in the crowd again. Her hair was hidden beneath a green wool hat. The color probably did awesome things for her eyes. She had hazel eyes, which seemed to change color all the time. More than once, he'd resisted the desire to just stare into them. She always wore her hair in a ponytail, and while he loved seeing the back of her neck, he'd wanted to untie it and spread it over her shoulders for as long as he could remember. It was wavy and kind of chestnut colored. He was always surprised that she kept it long, but maybe it saved money at the hairdresser. There had to be a logical reason.

Of course, Olivia was on time. Of course, she was doing the responsible thing. Spencer just wished she was a little more excited to see him.

It made him feel like a dick to be putting her out like

this. It would be three hours driving, easily, for her to take him home and then she had to get to wherever she'd been going in the first place.

How had Gabriel talked her into doing this?

Spencer smiled, though, as he walked toward her. "Gabriel just called," he said. "Explaining that he talked you into doing this drive. I can't figure it, though. Does he have charm that I don't know about?"

Olivia laughed lightly. Her eyes were green now. "Maybe I wanted to do it."

"I doubt that. It's a ton of driving."

"I don't mind. Really. And I'm already doing a ton of driving today."

"All the way home from Cambridge? On your own?"

"Yup." She stretched up and gave him a sisterly kiss on the cheek. Spencer thought it would be a bad move to give any sign that he'd be glad of more contact, given how long their drive together was going to be. "Welcome home."

Even knowing it might not have been a good idea, Spencer couldn't completely hide his reaction. Having Olivia so close was a temptation he couldn't deny. He turned into her kiss, treating himself to a deep breath of her scent and a nuzzle that might look accidental.

She didn't wear perfume. She smelled of moisturizer and soap, a clean scent that got him right where he lived. Everything about Olivia made him tight and hard. He met her gaze when she stepped back, worried that he'd given himself away. Her smile was still in place and he couldn't tell if she'd noticed his indulgence. "Thanks for giving me a ride."

"No problem."

"You're not going to drive all the way back here tonight, are you? It's supposed to snow."

Olivia gave him a look. "I like driving."

"Still, taking me home is a lot of extra time on the road for you."

"Not really. I'm going to stay at my mom's in Honey Hill tonight." She shrugged. "It's kind of on my way."

"But it's Monday tomorrow. Don't you have classes?"

"Nope. I fly out tomorrow night."

Spencer blinked. "Fly out?"

"I'm trading one Cambridge for the other one. I'm joining a research program in England as my post-grad work."

Olivia was leaving. Soon.

Really soon.

At least, she didn't have as much driving to do as he'd feared. That made Spencer feel better. "Oh. I feel better about the driving."

"Don't worry about it. My mom's expecting me."

They walked together toward the exit. "But your car doesn't run for free. Let me give you gas money at least."

"Gabriel already did."

"Still, it must have messed up your Sunday. Did you cancel a date for me?"

She laughed. "On a Sunday?"

"I thought you might be saying goodbye to someone before you left." He was fishing and he knew it, but Olivia didn't seem to get it.

"Not a chance of that," she said.

Spencer could have been pleased by that revelation, except that her attitude seemed to indicate that there was never going to be a love interest.

He must have misunderstood her.

He knew just about nothing about her love life, after all. Maybe some jerk had broken her heart.

She tugged on her gloves and he zipped up his

jacket as they approached the doors. He'd always thought she was the perfect size, small enough to tuck under his arm, light enough to carry, but curvy in all the right places. Sensible. Funny. Easy to get along with.

And smart. Wicked smart.

Too smart for him.

"You might have been at your mom's by now if you hadn't stopped here."

"Not me. I'm really not a morning person." She cast him a smile as they stepped into the night. "How was your vacation?"

"Not much of a vacation, helping Joshua pack up and move," Spencer admitted. "I hurt in places I didn't know I had." Was she interested in Joshua? He didn't want to think about that. "For a guy who likes to think he's footloose and free, he sure has a ton of stuff."

"You must have had *some* fun."

"Some, but it's good to be home," Spencer admitted and Olivia laughed again. Her eyes sparkled when she laughed, and she looked so mischievous that he wanted to kiss her.

As usual.

"Always the diplomat," she teased. "One day, Lexi's going to drag you off on vacation and she won't let you come home until you've surrendered all the secrets you keep hidden away."

Spencer was intrigued. "What secrets did she get out of you?"

"I'll never tell. It's bad enough that Lexi knows." She opened the back gate of a blue 4WD with a flourish before he could ask more. He put his bag in the back.

"Mindy," Spencer remembered. He found himself smiling, again, that she named her car.

"Mindy." Olivia frowned a little as she patted the car and he wondered what she wasn't saying.

"What are you going to do with Mindy while you're in England?" He thought she'd say that she was leaving the car at her mom's.

"I'm selling her. The guy's coming to get her tomorrow at my mom's."

Spencer was shocked. "I didn't think you could sell a car after you named it."

Olivia didn't smile. "It's stupid to keep it."

"Won't you be back?"

"I don't know."

That news was unsettling, but Spencer didn't comment. It wasn't his business, after all.

"All gassed up and ready to rock. Let's go."

Of course, she was prepared.

Olivia was a good driver and Spencer found himself quickly at ease. She should be a good driver—he was the one who'd taught her to drive a manual transmission, all those summers ago. She'd been wearing short shorts that day and he'd almost forgotten to watch the road. He watched her changing gears on this night and noticed how her coat opened, giving him a view of her legs.

That was a lot better than watching the road.

Some things didn't change.

They chatted as she left the airport and got on the highway. They caught up on mutual acquaintances in Honey Hill and talked about current events. One thing Spencer had always liked about Olivia was that she didn't make him feel dumb for not going to college. It was easy to talk to her, and her anecdotes about lab research made him smile.

"And now the bees," she said.

"The bees?"

"We're looking for genetic indicators that affect the transmission of parasites and disease. It's a huge project, because there are so many kinds of bees."

"And they're getting a lot of parasites now." Spencer knew the death of bees was a big problem.

"Exactly." Olivia nodded. "We need to work this out and save the bees."

Spencer thought of Honey Hill and the hives at the big house there. He knew that they'd seen population losses in recent years and there were several people—including Reyna—who were determined to fix that.

"Sounds like a great project," he said. "Worthwhile."

"Especially if we can make some progress. I'm excited about contributing."

Spencer wasn't sure he understood the details fully, but he liked how animated Olivia was when she talked about it. "It must be cool to be doing something that could change the world."

"Like you do?" she said with admiration.

"Me?"

"Wolfe Lodge is making a huge difference to Honey Hill. You and Gabriel should be proud of what you're accomplishing."

Spencer was pleased that she'd noticed. "It's not as big a deal as trying to save the bees."

"Ask some of the people who have jobs in Honey Hill now. They might disagree with you."

Spencer nodded, wondering when he'd see her again. The possibility of not seeing Olivia anytime soon made him want to spend every possible minute with her. "But the bees are calling."

"They're better than fruit flies," she said with a shake of her head. "I never want to research genetic markers with them again."

"Why?"

"They breed like nothing on earth." She changed gears as they approached Bangor. There was more traffic and a bit of snow was falling. He figured the roads might be getting slippery.

"Which presumably makes them good subjects for research on genetic markers."

"True, but you just get them sorted and start counting and they all take flight."

Spencer laughed at that.

She shook a finger at him. "Then some fool brings a banana for lunch and leaves it in the lab overnight. I've never seen so many fruit flies in my life."

Soon they left Bangor behind and the night seemed darker as they drove into the highlands. The forest was closer to the highway and the exits were less frequent. There were a lot fewer cars and Spencer heaved a sigh of relief when the road narrowed again, without meaning to do so.

"Glad I didn't kill you?" she teased.

"Glad to be in the country again. I'm not much for the big city lights. What about you?"

"I like both. And there aren't many universities with genetic research programs outside of cities."

"Cambridge this week."

Olivia nodded. "Then I'll have to see what kind of opportunities appear."

"There's the proof that you're the opposite of my sister. She'd be making her opportunities."

"Well, I'm not above sending some resumés and contacting some former profs. It's more a case of deciding what I want to do first."

"First or at all?"

"First. I want to do everything," she admitted with an ease that made him smile. "But is it smarter to teach first or to work in the field first or to do some more research first? I can't decide."

Spencer took a chance and asked what he wanted to

know. "No one special to sway your choices one way or the other?"

"No," Olivia admitted. "Not that there would be."

"Really?"

"Really. All that love stuff is just propaganda. I'm not above a little sex, but I want to accomplish something with my life, something more than having babies."

Spencer watched her for a moment, wondering if she was really as cool as that. "Not me. I'd be good with love, marriage, and babies," he said and she smiled. "Or no babies. I just never thought I'd be over thirty and single." Spencer grinned. "Neither did my mother."

"Never met the right girl?" Olivia asked.

"Just the opposite. I've met her but she's not interested."

The truck swerved a little then, probably because Olivia glanced at him so quickly. "Sorry!" she said and corrected her course. "You just surprised me."

"Why?"

"I don't know. I guess I thought you could have any woman you wanted."

Spencer shook his head, even though her compliment pleased him. "Well, it didn't work out that way. Maybe I should go back to school."

Olivia frowned. "And give up your success? Any woman who doesn't see what you've achieved in Honey Hill isn't worth having."

Spencer smiled at the endorsement. "Thanks, Olivia."

"It's true," she said, her color rising. "You've done a great thing there, creating jobs and opportunity in a small town that really needed both."

"It's just a bar and restaurant."

"And a menu that brings people in from miles around. I know that you and Gabriel have done a lot to invigorate that town. You're making a difference and that's awesome. Once you get the lodge renovated, the impact will be even bigger."

Spencer basked in her praise, all the more precious because it was unexpected. They drove in silence for a long while, and Spencer just enjoyed the sense of coming home. He'd get a fire started and just sit in front of it for a bit, staring into the flames. Too bad it was too cloudy to see the stars. The snow was falling harder now.

"You're going to come in, right?" he asked as Olivia took the exit.

"It's getting late."

"But you can't just drive me home and not let me say thanks."

She flicked a look at him that he couldn't read.

"Gabriel said he'd bring some groceries. Let me make you a cup of tea or cocoa, a sandwich."

"Just for a minute, though," Olivia said, to his relief. "I don't want to be too late getting to my mom's. She'll be waiting up."

"I'm not sure you should drive alone. It's colder and the snow is really coming down now."

It was true. It was almost all white outside and the road was already obscured. Spencer knew the plows would wait until the morning at this point.

"I could drive you," he offered. "And crash at the lodge tonight."

"Don't worry so much," she chided. "I have my phone and drive all over the place by myself."

"So, call me when you get to your mom's, just so I know."

She smiled. "Yes, big brother."

Spencer almost winced at the reminder, but instead

he made a joke. "It's a rotten job but someone's got to do it."

"I *have* a big brother."

"Yeah, well, I won't hold my breath on Brandon looking out for you."

Olivia laughed. "Me, neither." She peered at the road ahead, slowing down, and saving Spencer from an answer. "Which turn is it?"

"There." He pointed and she took the turn. "Then just up there on the left. The red mail box."

∼

IT WAS ALMOST TOO EASY.

Liv had expected Spencer to argue but he didn't. There was a two-track driveway through the forest to his cabin. She'd never been to his place and was curious to see it. She knew he'd bought the land and had it built after he and Gabriel had bought what was left of Wolfe Lodge, and understood that he'd done a lot of the work himself. The snow was coming down fast and thick. It made her feel as if she was driving into a Christmas card.

Well, if all went as it should, she'd be getting a gift soon.

Her heart skipped at that.

She felt Spencer's surprise that the lights were on, glowing in welcome.

"Who's here?" he muttered, but there were no vehicles parked in the driveway or carport.

"Maybe whoever was here left," Liv suggested, indicating the tire tracks in the snow. "You said Gabriel was going to drop off some groceries."

"But he wouldn't have left the lights on, and he shouldn't have left a fire burning untended." Spencer was out of her car as soon as she stopped. He took the stairs three at a time to the front door and she heard his keys. She took advantage of his departure to turn around and back into the carport to make departure easier for Lexi.

She also sent a text message to Lexi that they'd arrived.

Then she took a deep breath.

Here went nothing.

It was one hour.

She could make it count.

Spencer's place was bigger than a cabin but smaller than the rural retreats that many people built in the area. Olivia thought it looked like a one-bedroom bungalow. It was made of logs on a stone foundation and she could see the stone chimney rising from the middle of the peaked roof. There was a small porch on this side, but almost certainly a large deck on the other side.

She couldn't see the sky with all the snow coming down, but Liv figured there'd be a great view of the stars on a good night. It was quiet and the big flakes of snow were pretty. The forest came close to the house and driveway on three sides, making it seem as if there was no one in the vicinity.

Spencer had his own corner of the world here.

Lucky, lucky.

He came back out the door to get his bag from the truck. "Something else to chew Gabriel out about," he said with disgust. "He *did* leave a fire burning unattended."

"Well, it means the house is warm, anyway."

"It could have burned down. It would have served him right if I'd had to go live with him until I could build another."

"You worry too much."

"It's my house. It took a lot of time to build. I'd like to enjoy it a bit longer."

Liv laughed.

Spencer smiled at her and took a deep breath. "But forget Gabriel. Come on in. Name your poison and I'll make it for you before you go."

"Cocoa sounds great. Thanks."

"No guarantees on ingredients, but I can probably make you a sandwich, if you want."

"I'm fine, thanks. Just the cocoa."

They climbed the stairs to the porch as Liv's heart thundered and Spencer ushered her in with a flourish. "Well, welcome to my castle."

Liv looked around with curiosity. The furnishings were simple and unexpectedly modern. It was cozy, decorated in natural colors with the occasional touch of red. The opposite wall was all windows and even at night, Liv could see the snow on the forest.

The interior was dominated by the chimney of river stone that was in the middle of the house. They were standing in the larger section created by the fireplace wall, which had a kitchen and eating area as well as a pair of leather couches by the big windows facing the deck. Liv knew that on the opposite side of the fireplace was a bedroom with a four-poster bed, and a luxurious bathroom, because Lexi had told her.

Her mouth was dry and her palms were damp, but she hoped she was managing to hide her nervousness. Spencer took her coat and hung it up along with his own, and they left their boots by the door.

"It's a million degrees in here," Spencer grumbled. He tugged off his hoodie and cast it aside, giving Olivia a great view of the tight T-shirt he wore underneath. He strode toward the kitchen, then stopped to stare at a big red box on the counter.

Olivia swallowed. This was it.

"Open me," Spencer read from the tag, then glanced back at Olivia. She shrugged and tried to look innocent.

He eyed her for a minute and she knew he was going to ask her something, but his phone rang.

Saved by the bell.

"What kind of idiot move was that to leave a fire burning unattended in my house?" he said by way of greeting and Liv knew it was Gabriel. There was a flutter in her stomach, which she tried to quell by strolling around the main room. Spencer had some framed photographs on the walls and she pretended to be more interested in them than she was. "It's not unattended?" Spencer echoed. "What does that mean?" He looked around, as if seeking a guest he hadn't noticed.

Lexi and Reyna were here somewhere. That was the plan.

In the bedroom, obviously.

She just had to keep calm and do her part.

Spencer folded his arms across his chest and frowned, leaning back against the counter. "What if I don't want a surprise?" he asked.

There was a pause as Gabriel obviously argued with him.

"I don't *like* surprises," Spencer said. "It's a learned response. Lexi is my sister."

Liv smiled, because she was sure he expected that. He was watching her and she pointed to the door. "*I'll just go*," she mouthed, but he shook his head and straightened from the counter.

"You want me to open this box and put on whatever is in it." Spencer's skepticism was clear. "And you want me to do it now." He opened the box and peeked inside, as if uncertain what would jump out of it. Then he rolled his eyes. "It's a blindfold!"

There was a sound from the bedroom.

No, it was from the bathroom. Water splashed.

Spencer stared at the closed door. "Who is that?" he asked Gabriel in a whisper. "How can you be so sure I'll thank you for this surprise?" He listened, didn't look convinced. "What *have* you done to my truck?" He stared at the phone with such disgust that Liv knew Gabriel had ended the call. Spencer met Liv's gaze and she saw the back of his neck turn red. "Apparently, I have company to entertain."

"Lucky you." It was easy for Liv to act nervous. "I'll just go."

"No! That's not fair to you, Olivia." Spencer shoved a hand through his hair and looked so agitated that her heart squeezed. "I'll just see who it is and tell her to go."

"No! I think you should play along," Liv said. She took a deep breath and walked toward him. "I think Gabriel's gone to a lot of trouble to arrange this, and you should give it a try."

"But..."

"Whatever happened to your truck is done, and Cameron is probably fixing it so it's as good as new. Why not enjoy a gift when you get it?"

"What do you know about my truck?"

She shrugged, realizing her slip. "Nothing. You just said something about it. Cameron fixes everything, doesn't he?"

He still looked displeased, but it had to be his dislike of surprises.

"Blindfolds *are* kind of fun," she said as if she knew anything about it.

Spencer smiled slowly, an enticing heat dawning in his eyes. "Then you put it on."

Liv smiled back at him. "This is *your* surprise, not mine. Here. Let me help." She crossed the room, reached into the box and then put the blindfold on Spencer. It was a thick one, made of black velvet and padded, with a wide band of elastic to hold it in place. She made sure it was secure, then spun him around several times.

"Hey!" he protested, but she urged him toward the bedroom, spinning him as they went. Thank God it wasn't far.

"Olivia," he growled, a threat in his tone. God, she loved that he used her full name and when his voice was low like that, mm, there was no better sound in the world.

But she couldn't stop to savor it. He was going to fight her soon.

She pushed him harder.

"What's going on?"

"You're getting a surprise," Liv said, hoping she sounded calmer than she felt. "I'm helping."

Lexi and Reyna hurried out of the bathroom, both fully dressed. Lexi tripped Spencer right beside the bed.

Showtime.

"Hey!" he protested as he fell onto the mattress on his back. Liv followed him, bracing her knee on his chest to hold him down.

She heard Spencer catch his breath.

She felt him freeze.

And she used that moment of hesitation against him.

Reyna and Lexi had a pair of wrist shackles, which were tucked out of sight on the far side of the bed. Liv grabbed Spencer's left wrist and Reyna put a shackle on it. Lexi seized his right wrist and secured it at the same time. His wrists were bound to each other in nothing flat.

"Hey!" Spencer said again, but Reyna had already

secured the shackles to the bed frame. She shortened the bond, stretching his arms out, even as he fought against the restraint.

"Surprise, Spencer," Liv whispered to him. "I'm sorry I agreed to be part of the scheme."

"What scheme?" he demanded tugging so that his muscles pumped. He looked amazing. His voice rose and his muscles flexed, and Liv was afraid he'd break free.

"Gabriel's way of saying sorry about the truck." She dropped her voice to a whisper. "Your guest is here and ready for you. I'm going to go."

"But, Olivia..."

She dropped her fingertips to his mouth to silence him. "Hey, three's a crowd, Spencer." Liv kissed his cheek quickly. "Welcome home and have fun. I'll see you soon."

"But you're leaving!"

"See you sometime, then." She stood up and backed away. *One hour*, Liv mouthed to Lexi, tapping her watch.

Lexi grinned and held up two fingers. *Do it right*, she advised.

Reyna nudged Lexi and held up three fingers, her eyes sparkling.

No! That was too long! Liv couldn't argue because Spencer would hear her and they knew it. Lexi plucked the keys out of Liv's hand and Reyna gave her a thumbs-up, then Lexi slammed the door after they left. They giggled on the stairs and Liv wished they'd shut up.

Three hours.

No. They had to come back before then.

Liv locked the door after them, noticing how Spencer stiffened at that sound. This was it. She walked toward the bed, peeling off her clothes and letting them audibly drop as Lexi started Mindy and drove away.

Liv reminded herself that this was her wish come true.

This was her chance to let loose and indulge her every fantasy.

Maybe it would take three hours to be satisfied.

Spencer was hers for the taking and the taking should start now.

CHAPTER TWO

I t made no sense.

Who was in his house? Why had Gabriel fixed him up on this night, of all nights? Spencer had just started to think he might make some progress with Olivia, and now this. He wouldn't think about his truck. If Cameron couldn't fix it, Gabriel could buy him another. Having some woman seduce him wasn't going to change that.

Spencer didn't like surprises.

He didn't like being restrained.

He didn't like the blindfold.

All the same, it was kind of hot. He thought of Olivia saying blindfolds were fun and wished it had just been the two of them.

He heard her leave, which just about killed him.

But the other woman was still in the house, the one who had been in the bathroom. He thought she was the one who had tripped him into the bed, and he had to think that she couldn't be evil if Olivia had been convinced to help her tie him down.

It seemed a thin rationalization.

Had he heard *two* women giggle outside the door? That didn't make any sense.

Spencer thought about how he'd gotten into this situation. He thought about Olivia with her knee on his chest, and her capable fingers securing his blindfold. He thought about her being so close that he could have run his hand beneath her skirt if he hadn't been restrained, and his cock rose to attention.

He heard the woman bolt the door.

He heard her drop some item of clothing to the floor. A skirt? A pair of jeans? A bathrobe? There was no telling.

Something else joined it a moment later.

Whatever she was wearing, she was taking it off. That made her agenda pretty clear. What did she look like? Who was she? Why was he being deprived of a view? His erection was straining against his jeans by the time he felt the mattress dip beneath her weight. His heart skipped a beat that she was coming closer.

"Aren't you going to say anything?" he asked and his words sounded loud.

She chuckled softly, a confident sound that made him shiver.

He felt her fingertips on his thighs, and even through the denim, the weight of her touch made him shiver more. She ran the palm of her hand over his erection and he caught his breath. She caressed him, bringing him to attention with surprising ease.

Maybe it was really hot to be seduced like this.

He felt her tug the hem of his T-shirt free, then her hands slid beneath it. He felt her fingertips on his skin, soft and light. She caressed him as she pushed up the shirt. Her hands were soft and she spread her fingers wide to slide her hands over his ribs. Her touch was possessive and Spencer swallowed. She pinched his nipples a little as she pushed the cloth past them, then he felt her breath against his skin. She kissed his nipple, running her tongue in a circle of heat that traced the outline of his tattoo, and he felt her hair spill onto his chest.

Long hair. She had long hair.

And it was loose. Soft.

She had very very soft lips.

She grazed his nipple with her teeth, making him gasp, then blew on it so that it tightened. He felt the tip of her tongue as she licked the nipple, then she kissed and suckled it. He was moving restlessly by the time she repeated her attentions on the second, hard and ready.

Okay. Maybe this was an okay gift.

"You should have let me have a shower first," he said, well aware that he'd spent a long day traveling.

"You smell good," she murmured, and he thought there was something familiar about her voice. He reviewed all the women he knew, the ones with long hair, and couldn't imagine who would be convinced to do this at Gabriel's request.

The T-shirt was pushed higher, over his shoulders, baring his skin to her view. He felt her hair brush against his face, then her lips touched the pulse at his throat. The shirt was shoved up to bunch around his wrists and abandoned there, her hands roving over him as if she owned him. Her touch became more demanding then, and he hoped it was because she liked what she saw.

"Let me see?" he asked but she only gave that throaty laugh again.

She kissed his chin, and then the edge of his jaw, then his ear, her hands sliding endlessly over him. She was teasing him, her lips tantalizingly close but out of reach, her hair sliding over his face. He tried to catch her, but she evaded him easily. She leaned closer and he felt her breast against his side, then a shock of delight at the feel of her bare skin against his.

Of course. He'd heard her take off her clothes.

This *was* hot.

Her hand swept down then, her fingers easing under his belt. She made a little purr of pleasure that set him on fire. She moved quickly to straddle him and Spencer smelled her arousal before he felt her wetness touch his skin. He felt her feet beneath his shoulders and knew she had her back to him.

He growled and squirmed a little then, knowing that she was sitting on his chest nude and that he couldn't see what had to be a great view.

But she unfastened his belt with deft fingers. She eased his erection free, then pushed down his jeans and briefs, easing them over his hips and down his thighs. When her mouth closed over him, Spencer groaned with pleasure. Her lips were locked around him. Her tongue was driving him crazy. The smell of her arousal was almost enough to take him over the edge. She worked him slowly, drawing it out and making him simmer for release.

Who was she and what had he done to deserve such a welcome home?

Spencer was starting to think he should leave his truck with Gabriel every time he went away.

His hips were bucking when she straightened and he moaned as her lips released him.

"Not yet," she whispered and he couldn't recognize her voice.

"Let me see you," he begged and she only laughed again.

She left the bed and he was afraid she'd abandon him like that, hard as a rock and desperate for release. She removed his jeans, though, so that he was left nude. He heard the crinkle of a package and then she was back, her hands on his erection as she eased the condom over it. She took her time smoothing it on, teasing him with the promise of satisfaction. Spencer couldn't decide whether he wanted her to keep touching him or to take him right away. Her caress felt so good.

He'd definitely underestimated blindfolds.

She left and he groaned in complaint, only to hear that chuckle again.

He heard liquid pouring and was sure he could feel her looking at him. Then she was back, her weight making the mattress dip, her hands sliding over him again. He was glad to feel her nestling up beside him, her lips on his nipple, his throat, and then finally on his mouth. She tasted like wine, and her hands framed his face as their kiss turned passionate. Spencer turned toward her, wanting to pleasure her as well as be pleasured, and she caught her breath. He found his nose against her throat, his nostrils filled with the scent of her flesh.

It was a nuzzle just like a nuzzle he'd given only a few hours before.

And he knew this woman's scent.

Olivia.

Spencer thought of the feel of her hands, the curve of her breast, the touch of her hair, the smell of her against him, and his desire increased exponentially. Olivia! He had no idea why she'd done this.

And he didn't care.

He was going to make the most of the opportunity and ensure that she came back for more. Olivia reached up, sliding her hands up his arms in that endless caress. When her hands slid across his own, Spencer seized his moment.

He rolled suddenly to his stomach, trapping her partly beneath him, his thigh between her legs. At the same moment, he grasped her wrists, holding them captive in his own. He was bound, but she was caught. He braced his weight on his elbows, leaning on her just enough to keep her where he wanted her to be. She gasped and wriggled a little bit to find herself caught, which did just about nothing to reduce Spencer's desire. She was nude, her soft skin pressed against him from shoulder to hip and in a great many other places, too. Her hair was loose, and he wanted to see her more than he'd wanted anything in a long time.

"Time to change the rules," he murmured against her throat, then kissed her before she could argue.

Her lips parted beneath his, as if she would say something, but Spencer slanted his mouth over hers and deepened his kiss. She shivered, just a little, then opened her mouth to him, inviting him to take the only thing he'd ever wanted.

Olivia.

~

THE MAN'S kiss should come with a warning label.

Even tied down and blindfolded, Spencer was hardly at a disadvantage. He held Liv's wrists firmly, keeping her arms stretched above her head, and feasted on her mouth as if he was the one in charge. He was angled over her, his chest against hers, and Liv rubbed herself against him as he kissed her thoroughly. She liked the feel of his chest hair against her nipples, and the strength of his thigh between hers. His leg moved a little so that his erection was against her pubis and Liv writhed, wanting him to claim her completely. His kiss was hot and hungry, so passionate that Liv could have ordered it up on spec. She lifted her hips against him and felt him smile.

Then he eased between her thighs, sliding his erection through the wet folds of her labia. Liv caught her breath, wanting him inside her and tried to move so that she took him inside her.

Spencer pulled back and broke their kiss. He bent over her, whispering in her ear. "You like to tease, so I'm going to tease you back."

"No," she whispered, unsure how she could stand to wait for him.

"I want to eat you," he said and her eyes flew open.

"No," she said quickly.

"You don't like it?" He was kissing her throat and teasing her earlobe, setting her blood on fire.

"No," she admitted, trying to remember to disguise her voice.

"I like it," he growled. "I'll make sure you like it."

She shook her head and tried to pull her hands away.

"Then let me touch you," he whispered, before he kissed her slowly once again. He was taking control of their lovemaking in a way that Liv hadn't planned, but she had a hard time objecting to it.

He felt so good.

She shook her head again. "You're my captive," she said when he broke his kiss.

"I can tell," he said, his tone teasing. He pulled her up a bit and bent to take her nipple in his mouth. He sucked on it, and pulled it between his teeth, biting it gently so that she squirmed. His leg was over her thighs, holding her captive, as he turned his attention to the other nipple. His day's growth of beard prickled a little, but it felt good. Liv watched him, admiring how gentle he was and loving his attention to detail. She arched her back and closed her eyes, surrendering to sensation.

"You're wet," he whispered, when he returned to kiss her again.

Liv nodded. "Ready," she replied softly.

"Not quite," he argued, then put his lips against her ear. "I want you to come first," he said. "If I can't eat you or touch you, then you'll have to touch yourself."

Liv froze. Could she do that in front of him?

Not a chance.

But then, he wouldn't be able to see her do it.

Spencer rolled over her, bracing his weight over her more deliberately. All she could see was his broad shoulders and all she could feel was his chest holding her down. It was just about the most perfect place to be, except for one detail. She parted her legs and wrapped her thighs around his waist, trying to tempt him inside her. Spencer shivered, then kissed her again, a hard open-mouth kiss that left them both gasping. His erection was close but not close enough.

"You first," he growled and released one of her wrists.

It was her left one, fortunately, as Liv was left-handed.

She thought about it for a minute, then slipped her hand beneath them both. Spencer moved to give her access, then nuzzled her ear. "Are you wet?"

Liv nodded. "Yes."

"Slide your fingers over yourself and give me a taste." His voice was rough and that thrilled her.

Her gaze flicked to him, but he was serious, his lips in a line that was almost hard. She touched herself, shivering a little at the weight of her own hand, then brought her fingers to his mouth. He licked one fingertip, then slowly drew her finger into his mouth, sucking and licking it with a thoroughness that fascinated her. He did the same to the second one, sucking it thoroughly, then made a growl in his throat.

"Delicious," he whispered. "Feed me more."

She did it again, unable to ignore his enthusiasm. The scent of herself was surprisingly arousing, especially when she felt the effect of the scent upon Spencer. He was taut, a new tension in his body, and his erection seemed to have grown thicker and harder.

"Touch yourself," he commanded when he released her fingertips the second time. He bent to kiss her, then trailed kisses to her ear. His whisper made her shiver. "Tell me about your clitoris," he invited. "Is it hard?"

Liv swallowed and nodded. "Yes."

"Touch it."

She did, jumping a little at the weight of her own fingertip.

"If I touched you, I would draw a circle around it," Spencer murmured in her ear. "With my tongue or my fingertip. Do it."

Liv did as she was instructed and felt her mouth open as her excitement increased.

"And then I'd drag my fingertip across it, left to right, right to left, left to right."

Liv anticipated his command and did that, three times, each brush making her skin heat a little more.

"Then harder," Spencer growled. "Press on it."

Liv caught her breath as she followed his command. She squirmed a little beneath him and he chuckled.

"Lighter now. Tease it a bit. Around and around."

Liv's heart was racing.

"Now a little surprise. Press your fingernail against it."

She did and gasped, arching her back and tightening her legs around him.

"Give me a taste," Spencer demanded.

Liv's hand was shaking as she did what he instructed. He practically devoured her fingers, licking off every drop.

"Delicious," he purred. "You're ready for me."

"Oh yes."

"But you have to come first. Those are the rules."

Liv wasn't in a frame of mind to argue about who was making the rules. She wanted Spencer inside her as soon as possible.

"If I was eating you, I'd catch your clitoris between my teeth and suck on it."

Liv gasped, unable to imagine how that would feel. "I can't do that."

"You'll have to improvise. Tease it first, then catch it between finger and thumb."

Liv moaned at her own caress.

"Now pinch it, hard," Spencer commanded. Liv followed his instruction and the orgasm ripped through her with amazing power. She'd never come so big when she'd touched herself before, but she shouted and shook with her release. Spencer released her other hand and she clung to him, her nails digging into his back.

"Good," he murmured, holding her until her pulse slowed a bit. "Very good." She opened her mouth when she felt his erection slide against her labia, then arched her back when he eased inside her.

This time he trembled, but he moved into her slowly and steadily. He kissed her temple. "Okay?" His voice was husky.

She nodded. "I want all of you," she whispered and he made a sound of satisfaction. He moved back, then drove deeper, filling her and stretching her in a way that made her sigh with pleasure.

"I like your nails on my back," he whispered to her as he began to move. "I like the idea of you putting your mark on me."

Liv grabbed his shoulders, flexing her fingers so that her

nails dug into his skin. He moved faster, bracing himself a little higher on his elbows. She felt surrounded by him and filled by him, possessed and claimed. She felt her heart beat more quickly again and felt a flush of desire rise once again.

"Touch yourself again," he said, his voice hard with command. "I want to feel you come when I'm inside you."

Liv slid her hand between them and caught her clitoris between her two fingers. She pressed it and caressed it, sending a surge through her body at her own touch.

Spencer chuckled and she felt him get harder. He moved faster and deeper, claiming her as she'd never been claimed before. "Tonight, you're mine," he said and Liv thrilled at his words. She nodded and gripped his back, feeling the heat of his skin. "Pinch it again," he commanded. "Prove that you're mine."

Liv did exactly that. She pinched hard and a second wave of pleasure convulsed her with its strength. She cried out again, her legs locking around Spencer as he drove deep inside her. She dug her nails into his back as he buried his face in her throat and roared with his release.

Then he sank into her embrace, his breath quick and his skin slick with perspiration. He kissed her roughly, possessively, marvelously, then leaned his forehead on her shoulder. "Don't go anywhere," he murmured and Liv almost laughed. It would be impossible to do that when he was pinning her down with his weight, but she didn't want to leave. She ran her fingers through his hair and heard his breathing slow.

The moon had some fierce magic to share.

Her fantasy had come true, against her every expectation.

And there was just about no reason why it couldn't come true again.

She stayed still, enjoying the sound of Spencer dozing, content in a strange and wonderful way. The snow was falling more thickly outside the window, but Liv didn't care. She was right where she wanted to be.

~

SPENCER AWAKENED to the sound of water running.

He tried to open his eyes, but couldn't. That was when he remembered the blindfold.

He tried to move his hands, but couldn't. He remembered the shackles.

He remembered Olivia, too, and how she'd responded to him changing the rules.

Well, he was about to change them a little bit more.

She was in the bathroom from the sound of the water, and he guessed that he didn't have much time. He pulled himself toward his hands and managed to unfasten the blindfold. He shook it off, then rolled over, taking his teeth to the buckle on one wrist restraint. Once he had one wrist free, it was easy to unfasten the other. He shook off his T-shirt, which had been bunched around his wrists, and strode to the bathroom, the blindfold dangling from one finger.

Olivia was in front of the sink, gloriously nude with her hair loose. He could have just stared at her forever, but that would have to wait. She was washing herself with a face cloth, but Spencer stepped into the bathroom behind her and liked the way she started in surprise.

He plucked the cloth out of her hand, then bent to give her a kiss. "Come on. The shower's more fun." He reached past her to turn on the water in the shower stall, well aware that she was staring at him in shock.

"But..."

"You didn't think I was just going to stay there, did you?"

Olivia frowned as she considered him. Her eyes lit with understanding. "You let go of my *left* hand."

Spencer grinned, knowing exactly where she was going with that. "Coincidence?"

"You *knew*!"

"I knew." He offered his hand to her. "The water's hot, but it won't be for long. I don't have a big water tank here."

"You could have gotten away but you didn't?"

"I wanted to know what you had planned."

"That's sneaky!"

"This from the woman who tied me down and pretended to be someone else." Spencer arched a brow and Olivia laughed. She was obviously outraged, which made her look both cute and sexy as hell.

"Well, I didn't want you to know..."

"And now I do." He snapped the blindfold around her head and secured it, stealing a kiss when her lips parted in protest. "My turn," he whispered into her ear and she lowered her hands. "You're the one who said that blindfolds were fun."

"But it wasn't supposed to be like this," Olivia whispered.

"And it is. I changed the plan. You can tell me the original one later."

"Oh, I don't think so."

She was mortified, which was interesting. He'd never seen her so agitated.

"Weren't you going to tell me it was you?"

"Of course not!"

Spencer frowned. "Then what exactly was the plan?"

Olivia bit her lip, then cleared her throat. "You know, that. What we did. Maybe more of that."

"And then?"

"And then after an hour, Lexi was going to bring Mindy back and pick me up."

Spencer stared at her. "An hour? That's all?"

"Well, they said two or three hours before they left." She sighed. "You're not the only one changing the plan."

"And you're just going to leave?"

She nodded. "I'm sorry. I thought you would like it."

"I did like it. That's why I wouldn't want you to just drive away."

Her mouth worked in silence and Spencer couldn't resist the urge to kiss her again. She looked so vulnerable. So unlike her usual composed self.

And he *had* liked it. A lot.

The way he figured it, he had a little over two hours to convince her to give him more of a chance than this.

"Let's go with what's working for the moment," he whispered, then caught her lips with his. She leaned against him, as if grateful not to have to make any more confessions, and he felt his excitement rise again. They could talk later. He backed her into the shower, deepening his kiss, liking how she rose to her toes to respond. The hot water streamed over them, filling the bathroom with steam. It took her less than five seconds to melt against his chest, which suited Spencer just fine.

Things were off to an excellent start.

Olivia's enthusiasm took his breath away, but he knew the hot water tank would soon run dry.

"Hot water's wasting and I still owe you a cocoa," he whispered when he lifted his head. Olivia smiled, then reached out and licked his nipple. Her aim was off a bit, but he liked how playful she was. He lathered up with body wash and soaped her down, paying particular attention to her nipples. He held her against the tiled wall, cupping her breasts in his hands, then pinched her nipples. Olivia squirmed as he rolled them between his fingers and thumbs, then gasped.

"You're wicked!"

"I'm trying," Spencer admitted, stealing a slow kiss. He whispered in her ear, still teasing her. "I have this fantasy of hearing you scream when you come."

Olivia's cheeks were brilliant red and she wriggled in a very interesting way. "I shouldn't."

"Why not? Who's going to hear?"

"You will."

"And I'll like it a lot."

She laughed. "So, this night is about fantasies then?"

"It seems a good time to make a few come true. Was that one of yours?"

Her smile turned mischievous. "Tying you down and having my way with you?" She nodded. "Absolutely."

"So, now it's my turn. I want to hear you scream."

"You *are* wicked."

"You started it."

"True." Olivia took a deep breath. "All right. I won't hold back." She put out her hand for body wash and Spencer squirted some into her hand. She lathered it up between her palms, then spread it over his chest, working down to his erection. "Oh! Look what I found," she whispered, then began to caress him, working the lather over the length of him and cupping his balls in her hands.

Spencer leaned his head back and enjoyed. "Now who's wicked?" he asked, hearing the strain in his voice.

She laughed, a throaty sound that tempted him to

kiss her again. Her tongue slid between his teeth, sending a surge of desire through him, and he crushed her against the tile, kissing her deeply.

It was a few moments before he lifted his head and he ran a fingertip over her swollen lips. "Turn around. I haven't washed your back yet."

"And the water's starting to get cold," Olivia agreed, shivering as she turned. It was another great view, her butt sweetly curved and her waist so small that he couldn't keep from locking his hands around her. He lifted her to her toes and kissed the side of her neck, catching his breath when she rubbed her butt against him. "We should do it this way," she said to his surprise, her voice breathless.

"On your knees or against the wall?"

"I'm too short. I think it'll have to be over a chair."

"Your wish is my command," Spencer teased and she smiled, tipping her head back for a kiss.

"You should have told me that you take requests."

"Maybe I'm just at your service."

"Then why am I the one with the blindfold?"

"Maybe it helps."

She considered that. "Maybe it does. Maybe I can be a little wilder if I don't have to look you in the eye."

"I can work with that." He held her close, cupping one breast in his hand, then sliding the other hand down the length of her. She parted her legs to give him access and he was thrilled to feel how slick and wet she was. He loved how she moaned into his mouth, then shivered as the water got even colder.

"Time to finish up," he said.

"Tease," she accused.

"Don't worry. You'll get what you deserve."

She laughed again, that wonderful husky laugh, and Spencer got another handful of body wash. He pushed her hair aside and saw the tattoo for the first time. It was on the back of her left shoulder and still a little pink, as if it was new.

"What's this?" He ran a fingertip around its perimeter. "Is it new?" It was a bee in flight, approaching an open rose. It was just black, like a line drawing, except for the tiny red heart on the bee.

It was good work and Spencer admired it.

"I got it in New York," Olivia admitted.

Spencer nodded, knowing that she'd gone to Manhattan for a weekend with Lexi and Reyna recently. "To celebrate finishing your degree?"

She nodded, but she hesitated first, as if that wasn't the real reason.

"It's beautiful. Who was the artist?"

"Her name is Chynna."

Spencer whistled through his teeth. "A legend! Good for you. Why not go for the best for your first?"

"I kind of won it," Olivia admitted, as if embarrassed by it. "I didn't know who she was until later, when I looked her up."

He smiled down at her as he rinsed the lather from her body. He could have run his hands over her all night long, but the water was definitely getting chilly. He finished washing himself then turned off the water.

"You must be feeling lucky then," he murmured as he lifted her out of the shower. He wrapped her immediately in a huge bath towel and she nestled into it like a contented cat.

She smiled. "Actually, I am."

"Let me see if I can make you feel even more lucky."

"You just want to hear me scream."

"I do. And I want to eat you, too." He dropped his voice to a whisper. "That first taste was delicious."

Olivia didn't seem to know what to say. She reached to remove the blindfold, but he caught her hand in his.

"Not yet," he said. "You have to earn it."

"By screaming."

"Exactly." Spencer dried off and scooped her into his arms to carry her to the bed. "Reach up, way up, and grab the bed frame," he said. "You don't get to move."

"Or you'll tie me down?"

"Would you rather I did?"

She thought about it for a minute then shook her head. "No. I like the idea of capitulation."

Spencer grinned, then trailed a fingertip up the inside of her ankle. "Then spread your legs wide and don't move them until you come."

Olivia did what he instructed and pointed her toes. Her legs had the ideal amount of curve, to his thinking, and the towel was coming unwrapped around her waist. Her hair was a dark tangle beneath her and her lips were very red. Her skin was a bit pink from the shower and she smelled like body wash—and arousal.

Spencer took a good long look. It was his turn to see and he wasn't going to miss one bit of it. He eased his hand up her thigh and then felt the slick heat of her, liking that she was ready for him again.

And he was more than ready for a good taste.

∾

DESIRE MIGHT JUST BE an impulse to encourage the perpetuation of the species, but Liv had never realized it could be such a powerful force.

Or one that wasn't easily satisfied.

She apparently didn't even have to see Spencer to be excited by him. Being in his cabin, being in his presence, being in his shower and his bed, was evidently plenty. And even though they'd done it once, his kisses still turned her knees to butter. Clearly, it would take more than one or two rounds to satisfy her desire for him.

Fortunately, the urge seemed to be mutual.

And he didn't seem to be too angry about the trick she'd played on him.

At least not angry enough to hold it against her. Oh no, he seemed to be determined to change her mind about leaving, and Liv was enjoying his persuasiveness. Wearing the blindfold seemed to heighten her other senses and she felt his every touch as if it were magnified.

Plus, she could abandon her inhibitions when she didn't have to see his reaction.

No one had eaten Liv in a long time. It always made her feel self-conscious, possibly because she'd known that her former partners didn't enjoy it. It had been a reciprocal offer, if not an obligation, and that awareness had diminished Liv's enjoyment.

But Spencer seemed to love it. He took his time, easing his weight over her, sliding his hands up her thighs. She felt his lips on the inside of her knee first, a warm sweet kiss that made her shiver with delight, then his mouth worked a burning path higher and higher. She couldn't decide if the blindfold helped or hindered her reaction. She wasn't entirely certain what he'd do next, but on the other hand, that raised her awareness and anticipation. She felt each touch more keenly and that seemed to maximize its impact.

Liv would have liked to have studied her body's reactions, maybe compared and contrasted with the blindfold and without, but Spencer eased higher and she forgot everything except his touch.

She felt his breath against the inside of her thighs.

She felt his day's growth on her skin and shivered, expectant, impatient. He took his time, easing closer, teasing her with how slowly he could move. His hands cupped her butt, his forearms under her thighs, his shoulders on top of them. She felt his breath first and opened her legs wide, burning with need. He chuckled and that tickled, making her groan with impatience.

Finally, she felt his tongue on her labia. The slow, warm slide across her clitoris was heavenly. Luxurious. She felt pampered and indulged. Appreciated. Feminine. A whole list of things that she seldom felt and it was wonderful.

Liv moaned as she'd never moaned before. She felt Spencer grip her butt and make a little growl of satisfaction, then his tongue slid over her with deliberation. Liv felt dizzy. When he began to tease her, she wasn't sure how would last. He moved slowly though, building her up, then easing away, taking his time—as if he was enjoying it as much as she was. That realization nearly finished Liv.

"More," she complained, barely recognizing her own voice. "Faster."

"Patience is a virtue," Spencer said, teasing her with his fingertip. She knew he was looking at her, watching her reaction, so she slid her tongue over her own lips and arched her back. "No, I want to hear complete capitulation," he said, his voice low. Liv moaned and he chuckled, then closed his mouth over her again, demanding her reaction with his touch.

She knew what he was waiting for and she wished she had the ability to hold out. She tried to make the pleasure last, to keep herself from reaching her release too quickly, but Spencer seemed determined to drive her wild. Liv gasped. She writhed. She moaned and she felt her hips buck.

Then he touched her with his teeth and she screamed as the pleasure surged through her, screamed as she never had before. He didn't release her but kept teasing her, ensuring that she came and came and came.

She was out of breath when she tugged off the blindfold and threw it aside, then reached for him. His eyes flashed with blue fire, as he moved up the length of her, then he was inside her, hard and thick. His weight pressed her into the mattress and Liv wrapped herself around him, digging her fingers into his shoulders, drawing him closer and holding him tight. He rubbed against her, making her gasp in pleasure again, then his smile flashed. Their gazes locked and held and buried himself inside her, driving her back to the summit again. Liv felt the scream building again and knew that Spencer was waiting for it. She held back as long as she could, not wanting him to be cheated, but then the tumult overwhelmed her. She locked around him even as he buried himself deeply inside her, and screamed again as Spencer went taut.

He exhaled and she felt his heart racing beneath her hand. He lifted his head and kissed the corner of her mouth, a gesture of such tenderness that Liv's own heart squeezed tightly. "Cocoa?" he murmured and she couldn't keep herself from laughing.

CHAPTER THREE

Spencer heated milk and melted chocolate, trying to figure out the best way to change Olivia's thinking, and not have everything go straight to hell. Why did she only want one night? He knew her dad had died when she was young, and her mom had raised her and Brandon on her own, but he couldn't imagine that was the issue.

Maybe she only wanted to jump his bones.

Maybe the rest of him wasn't as interesting. She was brilliant, after all, and in possession of two graduate degrees. He'd barely finished high school.

But Spencer was stubborn and Olivia was in his cabin with no means of departure.

It was time for him to be persuasive.

The cocoa would help.

He'd tugged on a pair of jeans and a T-shirt but was barefoot in his kitchen. It wasn't a huge kitchen, not like the one at the lodge, but he had pretty much everything he needed close at hand.

Olivia was bundled up in a bathrobe she'd claimed from the back of the bathroom door. Lexi had given it to Spencer a few years before but he never wore it. No one had ever worn it, actually, but he kept it on the hook in the bathroom so Lexi would think her gift was being used. He was more likely to pull on a pair of sweatpants than wear a bathrobe.

It looked good on Olivia, though, all fluffy and white, a little bit too big. Once again, he thought she looked like a contented cat or a kitten, all snuggled up and cute as could be. She'd put her hair back in a pony-tail again and had borrowed a pair of his thick work socks. She was sitting at the counter, watching him. "Don't you use the powdered mix?" she asked.

"Bite your tongue," Spencer chided. "You need chocolate to make good cocoa."

"Is that how your mom made it?"

He shook his head. "She's a package-of-mix kind of woman, all the way."

Olivia smiled. "Mine, too."

"I learned to do this in France."

"At cooking school?"

"One of them." He swirled the chocolate into the warm milk, sparing her a smile. "I should give fair warning that once you've had it this way, you can't go back."

"Maybe *you* can't. I don't think so much about food."

"Good. I'll have a chance to change your mind."

"Just about cocoa?"

"Maybe about a lot of things." Their gazes locked and held for a moment and Spencer's heart stopped. Then Olivia caught her breath and looked down, her color rising.

So, she did feel guilty. Good.

"I've got an idea," he said. "Let's do a blind taste test. I've got one of those packages here someplace."

"More use for the blindfold?"

"Why not?" He grinned at her. "I like how you let go when you're wearing it."

"You just want to have your way with me. Again."

"I thought that was your plan," he teased.

She glanced toward the clock on the wall, which was all the reminder Spencer needed. Ninety minutes left. He had to get busy.

Alternatively, he could hope that Lexi was late, which wasn't out of the question. He considered the falling snow and wondered if it would even be possible for Lexi to drive back. How far had she gone?

"Okay, I have the blindfold," Olivia said.

"Put it on again."

She got back onto the stool, then put on the blindfold and tightened the strap. "Go ahead. Overwhelm me with better cocoa."

"I will. I'm going to use milk for both of them, just to level the playing field."

"My mom uses water with the mix."

"Right, so it will taste better this way, too." Spencer had warmed up two mugs because he'd planned to use half of the milk for his own cocoa. Instead, he made two kinds for Olivia. He poured milk over the powder and stirred it, then mixed some of the melted chocolate into the remaining warm milk. He poured the concoction into the other mug, sprinkled cocoa on the surface of both, then slid them across the counter to her. "Okay, this is the part where you prove me wrong."

Olivia smiled and reached out.

Spencer saw an accident just before it happened. "Hang on," he said, then moved around the counter to stand behind her. He wrapped his hands around hers, then fitted them around one mug, the one with the cocoa made with melted chocolate. She lifted her mug, wrapping her hands around its warmth, and he dropped his hands to her waist. She took a little sip to check the temperature. She gasped a little, then she took a bigger sip, and put down the mug. She ran her tongue over her lips, savoring it. "Okay. That's good," she said. "But it might be the milk."

"It might be," Spencer admitted. He guided her hands to the other mug and watched her hands close around it.

She sipped, considering, then sipped again. She put down the second mug. "I stand corrected. I want the first one back. It's amazing." She reached for the blind-fold, but Spencer caught her hands in his. "Why don't you leave it on for a while?"

"And put myself at your mercy?"

"Why not?"

She licked her lips as he watched and he knew the moment she capitulated. "Why not?" she whispered, her voice husky.

"You know where to come anytime you want another."

She smiled and something about her manner seemed a bit cooler to Spencer. "It would be a long way from England just for a cup of cocoa." She sipped again. "Although it is good."

"Too bad I didn't get one this way," he said. "Give me a taste?" She offered the mug to him but Spencer guided it down to the counter. "Not like that."

"But how...?"

He bent and brushed his lips across hers. He felt her shiver in response and heard her little exhalation of pleasure. "Like this," he murmured against her mouth and she turned immediately on the stool, her hands rising to his shoulders as she stretched toward him. Spencer kissed her deeply and thoroughly, loving how she met him more than halfway. That had to be progress on his part—she didn't seem very frosty to him in this moment. When he lifted his head, she smiled and slid her fingers into her hair.

"Now I should thank you for the cocoa," she whispered, which was fine by Spencer.

His hands were under the bathrobe by the time they broke their kiss and the smell of Olivia's arousal, warm and sweet, was leading his thoughts in a predictable direction. He eased his hand between her thighs and caressed her so that she gasped. He licked it from his fingertips, ensuring that she knew what he was doing. "Sweet as honey," he whispered and she smiled.

"You're insatiable."

"I thought that was you."

She shook her head. "I'm the Ice Queen, remember?"

"And I like how your reservations are melting."

Olivia straightened then and Spencer felt a barrier slide between them. "Not really. I have that flight tomorrow night. What time is it? How soon will Lexi be back?"

Spencer frowned. "You really don't have plans to come back to Honey Hill?"

"Like I said, there isn't a lot of post-grad work in genetics to be found out in the country."

Spencer looked around his cabin, looking for the right words but didn't find them. He decided to just dive in. "So, what's going on here, exactly?"

"A one-night stand," Olivia replied. There was a catch in her voice, as if she couldn't believe what she was doing. She pushed off the blindfold and put it down on the counter. She didn't meet his gaze, though, but reached for the mugs. Spencer didn't tell her which was which.

"An hour, or even three, is a lot less than a night."

"I thought you'd figure it out if it was longer than that." She sipped the one from mix, frowned and put it aside, then wrapped her hands around the other mug. She took a deep breath, inhaling the scent of the cocoa as if they weren't discussing something important.

Then she flicked a glance at him, her eyes very green, and Spencer knew she was just pretending not to care.

It was defensive.

But why?

"I thought this was a beginning," he said with care.

She shook her head, resolute in a way he didn't appreciate. "I thought it was a one-off."

"Why would you want that?"

"Because I wanted to *know* before I left."

"Know what?"

"Know what it was like to be with you." She sipped her cocoa and smiled tightly. "It was a lot better than I ever imagined it could be. Thanks."

Spencer was annoyed by her confession. "Then why are you leaving? Why not stay and make something of it? Why not give us a chance?"

She seemed to be puzzled by his question. "Because we did it. Because it was good. Because I'm booked to go to England and continue my work."

"I thought you might change your mind."

"That would make no sense."

"I don't think leaving makes any sense, not when even you admit it was really good."

Olivia finished her cocoa and put down the mug. "But nothing is static, Spencer. It can't stay good. Nothing lasts forever."

"I think love does last forever. Or it can."

"Love?" She shook her head. "No, nothing lasts forever, *especially* love. Even this cocoa is gone. It was great and I loved it, but it's gone." She pushed the mug closer. "Even if you made me another, exactly the same way, it wouldn't be as good as this one was. It's the first experience that has the power. After that, everything fades. It's inevitable. It's how life works." She held his gaze, completely convinced of her view.

Spencer felt irritable. "That's the most defeatist thing I've ever heard."

"No, it isn't. It's the way we're made. We crave new sensations. We seek new opportunities and experiences. It's what helps us to learn and to invent and to live fulfilled lives."

"I'd argue that without love, it would be hard to live a fulfilled life."

Olivia smiled. "Then we disagree." She was a lot more comfortable with that than he was.

"Does that even apply to making love?" Spencer asked.

"Especially making love!" Olivia said. "Attraction is the urge that compels us to mate. It's about the continuation of the species. We're attracted to someone, we become intimate, maybe there's a child, but either way, the attraction fades. It's served its purpose. Genetic diversity is encouraged by multiple partners so we find different people attractive all the time. Nothing is static."

"That's the most depressing philosophy I've ever heard."

"It's not depressing. It's reality." She leaned closer. "What's depressing is when people put a romantic gloss on what's really just sexual desire. They pretend or hope that something will last forever that's been designed to be fleeting. You can't hope for something to be more than it is. It is what it is, and we should face that. Spending your whole life with someone because once upon a time you thought he or she was sexy is a sad prospect. Sticking together because you had kids together is even worse."

Spencer was startled. "So, the whole family life is a false construct?"

"In a way. It might be a survival mechanism—two parents can care for and defend children better than just one—but in our society, we don't need that construct anymore."

Her argument made Spencer feel as grumpy as the steady passing of time. One hour was all he had left. "But I think love lasts forever. My parents are still in love with each other."

"Are they? Or have they made a life together? Does it make more sense for them to be together, economically and socially, than to be apart? I'll believe that, but I don't believe in enduring love."

"So, this was about sex?"

Olivia nodded. "Great sex as it turned out."

"And scratching an itch?"

She grimaced. "Exploring a fantasy sounds better."

"And so, as far as you're concerned, it's over."

She nodded. Her gaze flicked to the clock again, and Spencer had the urge to smash it to bits.

He had one hour.

He was going to make it count.

"How about starting an experiment?" he said, hearing the challenge in his voice.

"An experiment?"

"Let's quantify how long attraction lasts."

"It's done."

"Is it?" Spencer leaned closer and noticed how Olivia inhaled. "Because you don't feel any attraction any more?" he murmured. "That wouldn't be rational. You know what it's like to be with me now, so you can't be curious."

"Exactly," Olivia agreed but she swallowed.

Ha.

"We've done it twice, and the second time, by your own logic, must have been less powerful."

Olivia's gaze slid from his. "Well, not exactly, because it was different..."

"Every posture gives desire a new chance?"

"Well, not exactly. You're twisting my words..."

"Tell me this. You were going to keep me blind-folded for three hours, then walk out that door, without giving me any clue it was you?"

She nodded, her expression wary.

"And go to England tomorrow?"

"I figured I could avoid you..."

"Because there's no future in it anyway?"

"No, because men are more in tune with that." To Olivia's credit, she looked miserable. "Lexi said you'd never know and you'd be fine with it, that it would be like a fantasy..."

"Not my fantasy."

"Sorry." She forced a smile. "On the upside, there's nothing wrong with your truck. That was just an excuse so I could pick you up at the airport..."

"Lexi's idea?" Spencer asked and she nodded. "It was a chicken-shit plan, Olivia, a make-trouble-and-run scheme that's typical of Lexi but not you. I expect better of you."

"Really?" She seemed to be surprised. "I didn't think you had any expectations of me."

"I have plenty. Intelligence. Honesty. Integrity. A fighting chance."

"But, Spencer, there's nothing to fight for..."

"Wrong. There's *everything* to fight for here."

"No, Spencer, no. I'm sorry. I was wrong. I shouldn't have listened to Lexi. I'm sorry that I tricked you. But that's not the same as believing in love and be-ginnings and happy-ever-after and all that stuff that isn't real!" Olivia got to her feet, her eyes filled with the fire of her conviction. They were even greener now. "Love is a fiction. A fantasy wrapped around a biological urge. Believing in that is only going to lead to disappointment..."

"That's a load of shit," Spencer murmured, inter-rupting her. When she fell silent, he tugged off his T-shirt. "I say we go for the experiment."

Olivia's eyes widened but she took a good look.

He saw her swallow again.

"It's perfectly rational..." she began, but Spencer prowled around the end of the counter. She took a step back and almost stumbled, but he caught her arm and steadied her. She stared up at him, and flushed again. "It was just a last chance."

"It was a beginning," Spencer corrected with re-solve. "And I'm going to prove it to you."

She had time to part her lips but apparently couldn't think of an argument. That was fine by Spencer.

He didn't want to talk.

"You're wet and I know it," he whispered. "You're aroused, even though your desire for me should have run its course."

Olivia swallowed but she didn't argue.

"I've got an hour and I'm going to change your mind," he whispered and her eyes widened. Then he bent down and captured her lips beneath his own, smiling into their kiss when Olivia shivered, then opened her mouth to him.

∼

THINGS WEREN'T QUITE GOING as Liv had planned.

She did feel bad about tricking Spencer, but she felt a lot worse about his determination to prove his romantic goals to be right. This couldn't lead anywhere good. The problem was that she couldn't resist him. She couldn't even summon a logical argument, not when he kissed her as if the world was ending and he wanted to get as much of a taste of her as possible before it was too late.

It started with a kiss that made her forget all her inhibitions—again—and then his hands were inside the bathrobe and her breasts were against his bare chest, and there was only Spencer and the way he awakened her from head to toe. It wasn't fair that he was so good at feeding her desire, that he kissed as if he'd invented it, that she was all wet and ready to go again—that one taste of Spencer, or even two, was only making her want him even more.

It wasn't supposed to work this way.

The first time was supposed to be the most powerful experience.

It never had worked this way for Liv.

But Liv found herself on a leather couch, naked, with Spencer naked on top of her, and forgot everything about biology that she knew to be true. She rolled Spencer to his back and straddled him, noting the admiration in his eyes before she bent down to kiss him with every bit as much enthusiasm as he'd showed so far.

An experiment. The man knew her well enough to tempt her the right way. Well, taking off his shirt hadn't hurt either. And really, it would be good to know for sure that the attraction was fading and that there was a time when sex with him was less powerful.

It was only reasonable to test a hypothesis—Spencer

did something with his tongue right then that made Liv completely lose her train of thought. She heard herself moan. She heard him chuckle, then run his hand down the length of her. She shivered and moaned again, knowing she hadn't had nearly enough yet.

If she was going to get him out of her system, she'd do it right now. It was after midnight and she didn't have long until Lexi returned.

She was still leaving. Spencer wouldn't change her mind.

But Liv couldn't regret just how good it felt for them to be together.

Just once more.

∽

SPENCER HEARD the power go off.

More accurately, he heard the items that were on the grid go silent. The refrigerator stopped humming and it was probably the lack of that sound that woke him up. The nightlight he'd left in the socket in the bathroom for Olivia had also been extinguished. The shadows in his house felt velvety and intimate. Cozy.

Of course, having Olivia curled up against him, her breath fanning his chest, didn't hurt either. She was sound asleep, probably exhausted from their lovemaking and her long drive, and that made Spencer smile in the darkness.

He'd convince her yet.

Lexi was late, which really didn't surprise him.

There was a lot of light outside the windows, even though it was late. It had to be the glow of the snow. He heard the wind whistle in the chimney and left the bed with reluctance to stoke the fire. Fortunately, he'd brought in a load of wood before going to bed. In a few minutes, the fire was blazing high again, filling the cabin with orange light and warmth.

That made it seem even more romantic.

Spencer glanced out the window at the deck and saw that there was already at least two feet of snow. It was still falling with a vengeance. Maybe Lexi hadn't been able to come. He smiled, knowing that Olivia probably wouldn't be going anywhere anytime soon. That suited him just fine.

It would give him more time to change Olivia's mind.

Spencer could make sure of that. He retrieved his phone and called Lexi, who picked up right away. "Don't come," he said softly before she could say anything.

She laughed. "You know."

"I know. Don't come anytime soon."

Lexi sighed. "I'm kind of glad to hear that, actually. It took us almost an hour to get to the lodge and I thought we were going to get stuck."

"Mindy has four-wheel drive."

"I know, but it's good to have some clue where the road is." She paused for just a second. "It's going okay, then?"

"That's not your business."

"Even though I helped?"

"*Because* you helped."

Lexi laughed again. "That's mean. You're getting even by not telling me what I most want to know."

"Don't tell me you expected otherwise."

"No. Mr. Discretion does not kiss and tell." She sighed again. "Too bad, really. When should I come?"

"After the plows have been, whenever that is."

"Okay." There was a mumble in the background

and Spencer guessed that she was with Gabe. "Gabe wants to know if you're okay without your generator."

"We'll be fine. Look, would you call Olivia's mom? I don't want her waiting up and worrying."

"Already done, Mr. Responsible. I told her that Liv had fallen asleep when we stopped at the lodge for a bathroom break, and we agreed that was because of her long drive."

"Good thinking." Spencer was impressed that his sister had even thought of such a thing.

"It was Liv's plan, actually. She was going to crash at my place after I picked her up."

Spencer shook his head at this evidence that his sister was just the way he knew her to be. Some things didn't change. "All right. I'll see you when you get here."

"Right."

"And turn off your phone."

Lexi laughed again. "Oh, I'm unavailable. That'll drive Liv nuts."

"Then I'll have to help her find something to do."

"I want to know more!" Lexi complained.

"Go ask Gabe for inspiration," Spencer said, then ended the call. He'd deliberately kept his voice low and had called from the furthest point in the cabin from the bed, but crept back to check.

Olivia was still sleeping soundly.

She probably was exhausted from the long drive.

He closed the door to the bedroom to ensure that he didn't disturb her and began to plan. He checked what Gabe had put in the fridge and consulted his inventory of the contents of the freezer. He had to use up the meat before it turned—and he planned to make meals that would seduce Olivia into surrendering to pleasure. She probably thought of eating as providing fuel to her body, not as an opportunity for pleasure and indulgence.

He'd change her mind about that, too.

In fact, maybe a culinary seduction would help with the romantic one.

Spencer couldn't wait. The way he saw it, he had a limited amount of time to convince Olivia to come back to Honey Hill and/or to give him a chance.

He had to make every minute count.

On the upside, he was feeling particularly persuasive, and the weather was definitely on his side.

∾

LIV AWAKENED ALONE in Spencer's bed. She was wearing a T-shirt that was far too big for her and the bed was warm. The windows were almost completely white and the house was very quiet.

She sat up, listening for some hint of where Spencer was. Had Lexi arrived? Had Spencer left with her?

It wouldn't have been completely unreasonable for him to have retaliated against her for her trick, but it would have been out of character. A chicken-shit trick pretty much summed it up. Liv was ashamed that she'd done such a thing to Spencer.

Somehow she had to make it up to him.

If he gave her a chance.

To her relief, there were faint sounds coming from the kitchen, then she heard footsteps on stairs. A door closed, then opened again.

He was here.

Liv got her phone and saw that she had a message from her mom. She listened to it and was glad that her mom believed she'd stayed with Lexi. At least Lexi had made that call. She'd have to call her back once she knew her plans.

She called Lexi but the call went straight to voice

mail. She didn't leave a message, but turned off her phone, trying to save the battery charge.

Too late. The phone died in her hand.

Was Lexi ducking her call? It didn't take a lot of imagination to figure out why that might be. Had it been Lexi's plan all along to leave Liv here until the morning?

Spencer was back in the kitchen, but she wanted to wash before facing him. Liv went into the bathroom and smiled when she discovered a fresh towel and facecloth set out beside the sink, with a new toothbrush still in the package on top. The window was covered with white, which had to be snow, and she couldn't see a thing outside. The room was colder than she remembered, and both taps were turned on slightly, with water dripping into both the tub and sink.

The power had to be off. That would explain why the house was so quiet.

She tried the tap and the water was cold enough to make her shiver. She put her hair in a ponytail, then brushed her teeth in the cold water and washed her face.

There was a knock at the door, and Liv opened it to find Spencer with a steaming copper pitcher. He was wearing jeans and heavy socks, and a Henley with the sleeves pushed up. "Thought you might like some hot water."

"Thanks." Liv tried to take it but he shook his head, so she stood back to let him into the bathroom. "Is the power off?"

He nodded as he got a big copper bowl out from under the sink. He set it on a cork base on the counter and poured some hot water into it, then put the pitcher on another cork base on the counter. "It went out just after midnight."

"Don't you have a generator?"

He gave her a look.

"You seem to always be prepared for everything. That's why I wondered."

Spencer grimaced. "I took it into Wolfe Lodge before Christmas when we had a power failure, and never brought it back."

"And Lexi didn't come back." It wasn't really a question. Liv knew she hadn't.

"I called and told her not to," Spencer admitted, raising a finger before Liv could protest. "Think about it. Even Mindy isn't going to make it down my drive when it's hip-deep in snow. It was smarter for Lexi to stay put."

Liv nodded reluctant understanding. Of course, he was protective of Lexi. She eyed him, wondering what he thought of the situation. She couldn't help feeling that she'd overstayed her welcome, especially as she'd invited herself, and she felt a little bit trapped.

"I'll miss my flight."

"It might be cancelled anyway. And you won't be able to sell your car for much if it's damaged," he reminded her and she forced a smile.

"Sorry." Liv decided to be blunt. "I wasn't planning to stay, and you can't have been planning to have a guest. I feel like I'm imposing."

His eyes were very bright blue, so bright that Liv couldn't look away. He seemed very large and masculine all of a sudden, almost filling the room, and that reminded her of everything they'd done. She felt a familiar tingle down low and her mouth went dry. That had to be because he was so serious and watching her so carefully. "Do you want to leave?" he asked softly.

"That was the plan."

"Because now that you've had your taste, you're

ready to move on?" He didn't seem to believe that, but she did think he wanted her to say it out loud.

She eyed him. "I don't want to inconvenience you."

"What if you're not?" Spencer asked and took a step closer. "What if I'm glad you're here?"

Liv's heart skipped. "You just want to change my mind."

"Guilty as charged." His lazy smile made her pulse skip as did the intent in his eyes. He brushed his lips across hers and Liv caught her breath. He smelled like toothpaste and soap, and the scent of fresh coffee clung to his clothes.

She tried to continue the conversation, as if she was unaffected by his proximity and his touch. "Are you glad about the snow?"

Spencer's smile broadened and she felt all shivery for a different reason. "I'm not the one who thinks one taste should be enough. I'm more than willing to try to convince you to give us more of a chance."

Liv swallowed. "It's not rational to hope for more."

"Much less for the next time to be even better?"

"Exactly." The word fell from her lips in a rush.

He surveyed her, then met her gaze again, his own eyes simmering. "Then you'd rather I didn't touch you?"

Liv couldn't lie. "I didn't say that."

"Because it would be good to be sure?"

"Experimentation is the only way to quantify a reaction. It's the best way to test a hypothesis."

Spencer chuckled. "So, I'm an experiment. Or this is."

"You did say you were planning to change my mind," Liv said. "So, my hypothesis is that attraction is fleeting and thus, unreliable."

"And mine is that attraction is a sign."

"A sign? What do you mean?"

"We're attracted to people who might make good partners, people who might be the ones we could love forever. I'm attracted to you because you're a good candidate."

"But how could you know for sure?" Liv was genuinely curious.

"We'd have to get to know each other better, then trust our instincts." He nodded. "Then, of course, each of us would have to be a good partner and feed the relationship, be honest, listen, all that good stuff."

"And how does that tie into sex." She blushed when he glanced from the discarded shackles to her. "Pun intended."

He pursed his lips as he thought. "I hypothesize that when we can't get enough of a specific person, then that's another sign."

"So, there's a whole row of signs."

"A process of greater commitment." He smiled. "When a sequence of hypotheses are proven correct."

Liv smiled at that. "That's good." She then continued, feeling bold. "It turns out we have time to do more testing."

"Tell me what you want," Spencer said, a little challenge in his voice.

"More," Liv admitted, her voice catching on the confession.

"Isn't that irrational?"

"Yes, but it's true all the same."

"So, my hypotheses are winning."

"So far, but it's early in the experiment."

Spencer bent to brush his lips across hers. "I like the sound of it being a very long one," he said, his breath so warm on her skin that she shivered. "You're cold," he murmured, raising one hand to cup her breast. His thumb eased across her nipple, teasing it to a tighter peak even through the cotton, then he pinched it between his finger and thumb. Liv closed her eyes and leaned back, welcoming his touch. "Tell me exactly what you want."

It seemed brazen to ask for it, but his caress brought the words to Liv's lips. "That," she confessed and his pinch tightened briefly. Liv arched her back. "And I want you to go down on me again."

"Just to prove that your pleasure wasn't an isolated incident?" He was teasing her and she knew it, but Liv didn't care—as long as he didn't stop.

"And to verify that the reaction can be more powerful each time in succession. That's your theory and I'm skeptical."

"So, you volunteer to be the test subject."

Liv laughed and opened her eyes, meeting his gaze. "All in the name of science," she said and he smiled.

"You haven't asked me what I want," he murmured.

"Then tell me."

"You," he said, a blaze in his eyes. He tugged the hem of the T-shirt. "Naked."

"You, too."

Spencer stepped back and pulled his shirt over his head, kicking off his jeans and everything else by the time Liv removed the T-shirt she was wearing. He held up a finger, then gave her a wicked smile. "One more thing," he said and ducked into the bedroom. He came back with the blindfold.

"But..." Liv protested, even as he put it on.

"It's supposed to heighten your other senses," he whispered in her ear. "Let's make sure."

Liv didn't argue, because she could already tell he was right. She felt like her nerve endings were alert, waiting for his first move. She was tingling all over and her nipples were tight. She was already wet, for goodness' sake, and she licked her lips in anticipation.

She heard the water splash, then Spencer guided her to the middle of the room with one hand. With the other, he ran the wet cloth over her, and she clung to his hand to keep her balance. The facecloth was soft and thick, much softer and thicker than the cheap ones Liv bought. The water was warm and there was a smooth lather that smelled of vanilla.

He started with the back of her neck, then moved the cloth over her shoulder and down to her breast. His hand was strong behind the cloth, massaging her as he washed her skin. The water ran in rivulets down to the floor and once again, Liv shivered in a delicious way. He washed her arms and her underarms, her back and her breasts, using lots of water and taking his time. It felt sensuous and decadent to have him do this. Inefficient. Wonderful.

He rinsed her skin, then poured more hot water. She heard him squeeze out the cloth, then felt its heat land on her skin again. He eased it down her belly and she inhaled, knowing what he'd wash next.

"You should hurry," she said, hearing that she was breathless.

"Why? We have lots of time, and I'm enjoying this."

He raised the cloth to her nipple, caressing it so that Liv arched her back. She felt her lips part and heard herself gasp, then Spencer was kissing her. He released her other hand and locked his arm around her waist, holding her tightly against him as his mouth slanted across hers. He did taste like toothpaste and he felt strong even though his touch was both gentle and persistent. He teased that nipple to a peak, making Liv writhe against him, then she felt him smile.

His hand slid down the length of her in a bold caress, then slipped between her thighs. She gasped when the warm cloth eased over her labia, then moaned when he began to pinch her clitoris. The cloth was just rough enough to drive her crazy and she found herself on her toes, her hands locked around his neck. She pressed against him, rubbing herself against his erection, and heard him catch his breath. Maybe it was because she couldn't see his reaction, but Liv felt that she could act on her need. She wrapped one leg around his waist, giving him greater access, and felt Spencer's heart skip.

"Tell me what you want," he demanded against her throat, his voice a low growl.

"I want you to eat me," she confessed.

"I thought you didn't like it." He was alternatively pressing on her clitoris and flicking against it, the combination making Liv squirm with desire.

"I like when you do it," she admitted, knowing that she was blushing. "I like how you do it."

"Why? What do you like about it?"

"I like your tongue. I like your teeth. I like the way you tease me and pinch me." He dropped the cloth and slid his fingers inside her, working her clitoris with his thumb. Liv shuddered from head to toe, but knew what he wanted. "I liked when you made me touch myself and give you a taste."

His hand moved and she almost whimpered that his touch was gone. Then she smelled her own arousal and knew he was licking his own fingers. "Delicious," he murmured again, then kissed her. "Tell me what it's like."

"Like honey. Thick and sweet."

"Exactly," Spencer growled and spun her around. He wrapped her in that same luxurious bathrobe, his hands moving so quickly that she couldn't anticipate him. Then he picked her up and she knew because the air was warming that he'd carried her back into the bedroom. She fell onto the bed, then he followed her, crawling up the length of her with intent. "Invite me," he demanded and Liv spread her legs wide. She pushed back the robe, displaying herself to him in a way that would have been impossible if she hadn't been blindfolded.

He made a little growl of satisfaction, then his hands slid up her thighs. He braced himself over her, and she felt the warmth of his breath right before his mouth closed over her with resolve. Liv moaned and surrendered to his touch, knowing he would give her exactly what she wanted.

And even a little more.

Maybe her hunger for Spencer was a learned response to stimulus.

$\sim$

IF ANYTHING, Olivia was wetter and sweeter each time they made love. Spencer knew it was because she was feeling more at ease with him, which meant their encounters were becoming more honest and intimate. They were approaching the sweet spot, where each time would be both a revelation and a satisfaction—he wanted not just to get there but to remain there for the duration.

With Olivia.

He wanted her too much this time to tease her over and over again. If anything, his appetite for the feast she offered was becoming more intense. He took her to the cusp once, then ensured that she found her pleasure, taking great satisfaction from the way she cried out in her release.

He didn't give her long to savor it, though. He

wanted her too much. He wiped his mouth, then caught her up in his arms and kissed her, carrying her to the large leather chair in the main room. She was on her feet, tipped over the back of it in a heartbeat, her giggle telling him that she was more than pleased with his choice. She removed the robe and threw it aside, and Spencer enjoyed the view. He watched Olivia spread her hands over the leather, fingers outstretched as she savored the smoothness of it, and wondered if she was learning the power of sensation after all. Then she moved her feet apart and lifted her butt toward him, rising to her toes. She was completely compliant and so wet that he was afraid he'd come too fast.

He gripped her hips and lifted her slightly, sliding himself through the folds of her labia so that she shivered in anticipation. He eased inside her slick heat and she sighed with satisfaction, then wriggled against him.

"Okay?" she asked.

"Fantastic. Okay for you?"

She moved back against him again and Spencer caught his breath. "Oh, yes." There was such satisfaction in her voice that he smiled.

And he knew how he could improve that. He moved, easing deeper then out again, then slid one hand beneath her. He let his fingers ease through her pubic hair to her clitoris and she tensed for a moment.

"I don't think I can again. Not so soon," she whispered, the tension in her voice indicating otherwise.

"Let's find out," Spencer said, teasing her clitoris as he moved. He closed his own eyes, lost in the pleasure that was Olivia.

"All in the interest of science," she said, then her voice caught and neither of them said anything articulate for a while.

CHAPTER FOUR

L iv couldn't understand it.

She watched Spencer organizing produce on the counter, fascinated by her own reaction to the sight.

She wanted him. Again.

Still.

Despite having had him multiple times.

If anything, she wanted him more than she had the day before. Her appetite was far from exhausted: it was stronger.

That was incomprehensible. She watched him, wondering if she could be wrong and he could be right.

Spencer was working on the far side of the counter, moving with efficiency. There was a line of small bowls down the middle of the counter, all the same white ceramic but of different sizes.

Liv was more interested in Spencer than what he was doing. They'd washed up together and dressed again, Spencer putting on the same clothes as earlier. He'd loaned Liv a sweatshirt, but she was wearing her own jeans and underwear. She wished she had another pair, but was glad that Spencer didn't have a stash of women's underclothes as part of his preparation for guests.

He flashed her a smile. "Coffee?"

"Please."

She watched his hands as he poured it into a mug from a pot on the stove, added a swirl of milk, then pushed it across the counter to her. It was nice that he remembered how she preferred her coffee. She sipped and was astonished by the powerful flavor. It was as if her senses had been suddenly turned on after slumbering for all of her life. She tasted it again and it was just as delicious.

"Good?" he asked, obviously noting her reaction.

"Amazing," Liv admitted. "Best ever."

"Fresh ground beans," Spencer said, his tone matter-of-fact. "I had to use the hand grinder this morning."

Liv nodded, knowing then what the unfamiliar sound had been. She took another sip and felt the coffee's heat flood through her. Everything had changed, as if she'd been awakened. "Are you going to tell me that this is like the cocoa? That there's no going back?"

He laughed and she knew he liked the idea. "Maybe you're going to tell me that."

"Maybe I just really needed a coffee," she said, her tone teasing as she slid onto a stool to watch him.

"Maybe you're paying more attention now."

Because of the blindfold. Liv felt like she was starting to blush again and knew Spencer was watching. She closed her eyes and took another sip, letting the coffee roll over her tongue. It really was the best cup she'd ever had.

Maybe it was because her senses were sharper, even without the blindfold.

Spencer had an expression of satisfaction when she opened her eyes again and Liv put the cup down on the counter, keeping her hands wrapped around it. "Maybe I'll get hooked on it."

"You know where to come for more."

"Maybe that's your diabolical plan."

"It wasn't, but it's not a bad idea." His gaze warmed. "I could get used to you coming around for coffee. And more."

Liv didn't know what to say to that. This wasn't permanent or even ongoing and she didn't want to suggest otherwise. She was going to England. And probably not coming back soon—if ever.

For the first time, Liv wondered if that really was such a great plan. She loved being in the research lab and doing the hard work to back up a theory, but the prospect of months alone seemed a little less appealing this morning.

She watched Spencer work and noticed a thousand little details about him, things she'd never paid attention to before. His eyelashes were thick and dark, which made his eyes look more blue. He had a tiny dimple below the corner of his mouth, one that appeared so rarely that she wasn't surprised she hadn't seen it before. His eyes brightened in color when he was intent, as he was now. His hands were strong and capable and it was all too easy to remember the sight—and the feel—of them on her skin.

The fridge door was open slightly and she guessed that it was empty. The power was off, after all. "What's in that box?" she asked, pointing to the box by the door. It was white cardboard, like a box from a bakery.

Spencer made a face. "Cupcakes left too close to the fire for too long."

"Oh! They must be Reyna's."

"And not a pretty sight."

"Let's not tell her."

He spared her a glance that spoke volumes.

"What did you do with everything from the fridge?"

"The basement is colder, so I loaded a couple of coolers down there with the perishables. We'll have to eat our way through things."

"That's not much of a break for you."

"I love cooking," he said, and she heard the truth of that in his tone.

"This looks really organized, like laying out the materials for a procedure in advance." Liv said, gesturing to the line of bowls.

"*Mise en place*," Spencer said.

Liv didn't understand but she recognized the phrase. "That's what your tattoo says." She indicated the image on his forearm of a chef's knife with those words beneath it in script. "What does it mean?"

"Put in place or, more loosely, have everything in its place. It means you do all the preparation before you start to cook. Then the process of preparing the meal goes more smoothly."

"Because you don't have to run off and wash a tomato." She nodded. She worked exactly the same way in the lab. "That makes sense. Is that what your tattoo means or is it a philosophy?"

Spencer smiled. He had a full sleeve on his left arm, starting with the *Mise en place* one just above his wrist. "Both. I got it to commemorate my first cooking course."

"And the leaves?" Liv indicated the tattoo on his upper arm. Each stem in the cluster was from a different plant, since their leaves were different.

"A *bouquet garni*, which I got after my first course in France."

"What's a *bouquet garni* for?"

"It's a cluster of herbs added to flavor the sauce or the stock. The French use a specific combination of herbs." He pointed to each one in his tattoo. "Parsley, bay, sage, thyme, rosemary. You can also add chervil, savory, and tarragon. The bundle is tied with leek leaves. The *bouquet garni* cooks with the stock or gravy, then is removed before the dish is finished."

It sounded fussy and complicated to Liv. "Is it worth it?"

"Absolutely." He must have noticed her expression because he smiled. "It makes all the difference."

"Salt and pepper is the extent of my additions."

"Ketchup?"

"No."

"There's hope then," he teased. "In Provence, they add peppercorns, other whole spices, or some dried orange peel."

"You can't tie those in a bundle."

"No. Some people use a muslin bag then, because they want to fish them out before serving."

"Why?"

"Ever bitten into a peppercorn?"

Liv smiled. The rest of his tattoo sleeve was composed of vegetables and fruits, scattered around his arm like a display at a farmers' market. "Those would be your farm-fresh ingredients."

"They're all heritage varieties."

"Because you like cooking with them best?"

"Because farm-to-table is a big part of what I do and what we do at the lodge, plus sourcing food locally and supporting more regional suppliers. We use artisan cheeses whenever we can, for example, as well as local produce and meat. We even have a few foragers who bring in fiddleheads, garlic scapes, and mushrooms when they're in season. It makes our menu distinct and local."

More curious, Liv leaned forward to look in the bowls. She recognized baby spinach leaves in the biggest one, diced nuts in a smaller one, a crumbled white cheese in another. There were several small bowls with what looked like oil in them and she guessed that the quantities were measured. As she watched, Spencer took a whisk to one of them and poured another liquid into it slowly as he mixed the contents. He tasted the result, then added a pinch of what might have been salt from an open bowl, then ground pepper into it. When he tasted it this time, he nodded, then set it in the line.

There was a pear and four big oranges, still awaiting his attention, as well as brown eggs and a stick of butter. He broke the eggs into a pitcher, then broke three more and separated the yolks. Liv watched, fascinated. It was like magic, but he made it look easy. He whisked the yolks and she surveyed his preparations again. She was starting to realize that she was hungry. A round loaf of bread that might have been sourdough was at the end of the counter and at the other end, a brown paper bag with the top folded down.

Liv peered into it and the scent of seaweed made her step back. "Is that a lobster?"

"Yes. Two of them actually."

She looked again. They were both dark, between green and black in color, and had bands around their claws. They were moving a little.

"Are they alive?"

"Not for much longer."

"Because they're not in the ocean?"

"No. They're cold and in a bit of seaweed. They were probably harvested yesterday. They're going to die because we're going to eat them."

She understood then why there was such a large pot on the wood stove. Steam was beginning to rise from it.

"Do you always have lobster in your fridge?" They were in Maine, but still, it seemed strange to Liv. Luxurious.

Spencer's grin flashed. "No. You can thank Gabriel for that."

"Oh, I forgot. He was buying you some groceries."

"And he was part of *your* plan." Spencer indicated the food on the counter. "You see before you all of the required ingredients for number two of Gabriel's *Seven Romantic Meals Guaranteed to Get You Lucky*."

Liv laughed in surprise. "Really?"

"Really. He has a blog and Instagram account for the lodge. These articles get him tons of traffic."

"It's a catchy title."

"I made him change *Laid* to *Lucky*."

Liv laughed. "It doesn't seem like you need any help getting lucky right now."

"No." Spencer smiled at her. "Do you?"

"No," Liv admitted with a blush.

"Gabriel must have thought we'd need help."

Neither of them commented on that. Liv cleared her throat. "So, what are the seven meals?"

"Eggs Benedict with Lobster is the one we'll start with. Then there's Scallops with Spinach and Risotto. I think we'll have that tonight."

Liv nodded. "The shellfish get eaten first."

"There's going to be enough lobster left for lobster mac and cheese, but once it's cooked, it'll keep longer."

"Then?"

"I haven't decided. The whole chicken should probably be eaten next, but do you have any preferences or allergies?"

Liv shook her head. "I eat whatever's going."

"You have to be more particular than that."

"Not really. You're going to think I'm weird, but I don't pay that much attention to food." She savored another sip of her coffee and wondered if that was changing.

He gave her a look. "But you cook, right?"

"No."

That startled him. "But you must cook something. I mean, you don't have to be a chef to say that you cook."

"I don't."

"You don't cook *anything*?"

Liv felt a bit defensive. "I heat things up. Cans of soup. Frozen entrées. I get prepared stuff at the grocery store, because it's better than eating take-out all the time."

Spencer stared at her in astonishment. "Didn't Audrey cook?" he asked, referring to her mom.

Liv had to shake her head again. "She taught me what I know. Frozen lasagna in the oven, salad mix in the bowl." She shrugged. "It's probably more common than what you do."

"You have to know how to roast a chicken," Spencer said.

"No," Liv admitted. "When I want one, I buy it cooked at the grocery store."

"There's a depressing thought." He shoved a hand through his hair and surveyed the kitchen, apparently uncertain of what to say. He looked a bit beleaguered, as if Liv had shaken the foundations of his universe.

Maybe she had.

Fortunately, Liv had an idea how to set it to rights.

≈

SPENCER ALWAYS HAD a plan by the time he stepped into the kitchen, but on this day, the stakes were higher than usual—and they seemed to be getting higher by the minute. He'd known immediately that he had to ensure that he used the better food in his fridge before it spoiled. That was basic management. He'd also known that he wanted to impress a woman who didn't seem to have a lot of interest in food. Olivia's comments this morning, though, made him feel that this was an exercise in futility.

She didn't believe in love.

She didn't care about food.

He was doomed to lose the battle and the war.

"I always think of cooking as just more work," Olivia admitted. "As something that takes time." Spencer turned to look at her, unable to make sense of a philosophy so opposite to his own. She lifted her cup and saluted him before she finished her coffee. "But you're making me aware of the possibilities. Would you teach me to cook?"

Relief weakened Spencer's knees. "You want to know? You don't think it's a waste?"

"No. I guess I just never paid attention before."

"Mindfulness," he said. "Paying attention is a big part of eating well and enjoying it. Part of a lot of other pleasures, too."

Olivia smiled and his heart leaped at the sparkle in her eyes. "So I'm learning." Their gazes clung in that way that sent heat through him from head to toe, the way that made him want to forget about food and head back to the bedroom. "Go ahead," she said, a challenge in her tone. "Convert me."

Spencer was up for that. "Brunch is eggs benedict with lobster."

"Sounds fancy."

"Not really. It's actually simple." He gestured to the bowls on the counter. "Everything comes down to the ingredients being fresh and good."

"All right." Olivia looked unconvinced but willing to try. "What can I do?"

"Are you squeamish?"

"Not particularly. Why?"

He pointed to the lobsters. "Because they have to be cooked, then cleaned. They're not that pretty inside."

"I have an undergrad in biology," Olivia said, getting off the stool to move to his side of the counter. "Dissection has been my middle name for years." She spared him a look. "I won't faint or puke."

Spencer smiled. "I don't have any scalpels."

"I'll work with whatever sharp tools you've got. I'm flexible like that."

He chuckled. "Okay." Spencer took the lid off the pot of water, releasing the steam. He'd treat this like a class and try to spark her enthusiasm. "There's salt in the water, already," he told her. "That ensures the flavor."

"Why?"

"I had a teacher who said seafood needs to remember the sea. Salt is the key to that."

Olivia nodded understanding. "Not much water in there, though."

"A couple of inches. We're going to steam them." He put in the boiling rack.

"Why?"

"The meat is more tender and it's harder to overcook them." When Olivia nodded, Spencer reached into the paper bag and grabbed one lobster. "Always pick them up by the carapace." It moved more energetically once he grabbed it and its tail flicked hard.

"It's frisky."

"Which means it's freshly caught. When you look for one in the market, look for intact antenna. That's another sign of freshness. Go on, grab the other one."

Olivia did as instructed, echoing his move.

"Make sure it feels cold to the touch still."

"Another test?"

"Absolutely." He put the lobster down on the cutting board and drove his knife into the back of its head. Olivia looked startled. "It's called pithing them. It means they don't boil alive."

"A better choice," she said. Spencer stepped toward the pot and picked up a pair of scissors. He cut the rubber bands very quickly, flicking them to the counter, then dropped the lobster into the pot. Olivia let him take her lobster and watched him repeat his motions, then set the timer as instructed and put the lid back on.

"Things will get quicker now," he warned her.

"But everything's ready."

"Except the pear. I didn't do it sooner because it would turn brown. Could you cut it into eighths, then peel and core it? Leave the pieces in order if you can, so we can fan it out for the presentation."

She was quick to comply and he admired how deft she was with a knife.

That she didn't suggest that presentation was irrelevant had to be a good sign.

While the lobsters cooked, Spencer toasted the slices of bread on the stove and brought the water for the eggs to a boil. He had two plates already warming at the back of the stove, and had Olivia butter the toast. She also tossed the salad, mixing the spinach with the vinaigrette he'd already made.

"We'll add that last, like a garnish, because we don't want it to wilt in the heat."

She nodded understanding as he cut the oranges in half.

"If you could juice these, that would be great."

"Look at the color of them!" Olivia examined the fruit, taking an appreciative sniff. "These are so nice. I always seem to pick crummy ones."

"Look at the skin when you shop," Spencer said.

"The pores are small on these and the skin is smooth. It's a bit shiny, even. That means the interior is juicier than if the pulp is thick."

Olivia blinked. "So, you can tell what the inside is like even before you cut them open?"

"Exactly. When the pulp is thicker, the skin looks more lumpy and it has bigger pores. You want this kind of smooth shiny skin on all citrus. It's in season in the winter, so you have a better chance of getting good citrus at this time of year."

"Unless it's from the southern hemisphere."

"True. But then it isn't anywhere near local, and the shipping doesn't do it any favors."

Olivia juiced the oranges, filling the pitcher he'd provided with the juice. He'd put out two fluted glasses when he set the table in front of the fireplace and removed the bottle of prosecco from the cooler. The timer went and he put the lobsters in the sink in cold water to cool. They were bright red in color. He slipped the eggs into a pan of boiling water to poach.

"You've done that before," Olivia noted.

"A few thousand times," he admitted, then beckoned to her as he went to the sink.

"This would be the dissection bit," Olivia said.

"Exactly." The sink was wide enough for them to stand beside each other. Spencer could feel her warmth close beside him and knew he could easily get used to working together like this. He took one lobster in hand and twisted off the tail and claws with quick gestures. Olivia watched then did the same to hers. "Well done for a rookie," he teased and she laughed. He showed her how to slit the tail and remove the meat, which he put aside. Then he cracked the claws, which were big and rosy, and arranged the pieces on the toast.

"That's pretty," Olivia acknowledged, then did the

same with her lobster. She cut the intestinal veins out of the tails, and left that meat for later as Spencer instructed. She collected the waste in a bowl, definitely not squeamish, then washed her hands.

"Final approach now," he warned her. "This is the sprint to the finish."

She brushed her hands together. "I'm ready."

He'd already whisked the egg yolks and took the pitcher and whisk in hand again. The eggs were seconds from being done. He handed her a small pot of melted butter from the stove. "Can you pour the butter in a thin steady stream while I beat the sauce?"

Olivia followed his instructions. "How do you do this alone?"

"I use an immersion blender."

"I don't see one."

"It's at the lodge."

She laughed. "Good thing I'm here."

"It *is* a good thing," he said quietly and their gazes locked for a potent moment. He watched her swallow and drop her gaze and knew exactly what he wanted to do for the afternoon.

The hollandaise was perfect and the eggs were done. Spencer lifted each one from the water, placed it on a piece of toast, and brought the plates to the counter. He covered each egg with hollandaise, then arranged the salad beside it in a crescent, adding the slices of pear, walnuts and sprinkling of feta. A twist from the pepper mill and he was done. Olivia carried the plates to the table and sat down at his gesture.

"That's really attractive," she said, considering the plate in front of her with admiration.

"There's an old German proverb that one eats also with the eyes."

"I like that." She glanced around the room, the

white snow against the windows, the fire blazing, then her gaze landed upon him. "A feast for the senses," she said quietly, then smiled.

Spencer eased the cork from a bottle of prosecco, poured orange juice into fluted glasses, then added the prosecco. The mimosa sparkled and foamed as he offered her a glass.

Olivia lifted her glass. "Here's to the first seductive meal."

"Six more to go," Spencer said, hoping that the snow kept on falling as he touched his glass to hers.

"Are we going to get lucky seven times, or only at the end?" Olivia asked, her eyes dancing.

"I vote for seven times."

"Me, too." They toasted each other and the room seemed much warmer than it had been before.

It was only as Spencer tasted the mimosa that he wondered why he was teaching Olivia how to cook seven meals guaranteed to get her laid when she was leaving for England as soon as possible.

~

WITH ONE BITE, Liv knew that food would never be "just fuel" again.

She felt that if she looked in the dictionary under "decadent," there'd be a picture of her brunch. The lobster was firm and sweet and still warm. The toast was thick and crunchy beneath it, and she was sure she'd never tasted butter that was so rich. The hollandaise sauce was divine and when she broke the yolk of the egg, that just made the combination better. The salad was a little tart in contrast, probably from the vinaigrette, and she liked the combination of pear, walnut, and a little cheese. The prosecco bubbled on her tongue, the fresh sweet taste of orange juice an ideal complement to its tartness.

She found herself closing her eyes to take her second bite and letting the flavors explode in her mouth. She chewed slowly, savoring, knowing that Spencer had changed everything with one meal.

Had it been the coffee?

The cocoa?

The blindfold?

Either way, he'd been right—she knew there was no going back. Food would never be the same for her.

When she opened her eyes, Spencer was watching her, his eyes that intent blue. "It's amazing. Thank you."

"It's what I do," he said and took his own first bite. She watched how his gaze danced over his plate and knew he was assessing it more clinically that she had.

It was funny to think of herself as the emotional one.

It was interesting to see him assess the result of his work in much the same way as she would assess a completed protocol.

Maybe they weren't that different, after all.

"Are you giving it a score?" she asked and he grinned.

"Always. And looking for potential improvement."

Liv could relate to that. "What's the score out of ten?"

"With an allowance for the absence of my gas range, I'd say we've managed a nine." He saluted her with his glass and they sipped together. "A winning team."

Liv drank his toast. "Do you make eggs like this all the time?"

"Every Sunday, it's the brunch special at the lodge. People like it."

"I can see why."

They ate in satisfied silence for a few moments, the fire crackling beside them.

"Tell me about genetic markers," Spencer invited when his plate was clean.

"Why?"

"Because I don't understand what you do." He shrugged. "I might not understand it after you explain it, either, but give me a try."

"I can explain things better than that."

He leaned back, sipping his mimosa, eyes gleaming. "Go for it."

"You know about DNA, right?" She drew a double spiral on the table with her fingertip, and Spencer nodded.

"The double helix.

"Deoxyribonucleic acid," she confirmed. "The chain of genetic instructions."

"For replicating cells."

"Right. We have a particular style of DNA as a species, with twenty-three chromosomes, DNA that makes humans look the way we do. Then there's individual variation. Yours is a combination of the DNA of both of your parents, but it's your personal mix. It's similar but a bit different from Lexi's DNA."

Spencer nodded, then refilled their glasses. "Lexi and I both have dark hair, but her eyes are more grey, like those of my paternal grandmother."

"Exactly! And that's just one of the differences between you."

"Gender."

"I noticed that," Liv said and they shared a smile. "Everything that makes you you is coded in your DNA." She indicated her drawing. "The two DNA strands are composed of simpler structures called nucleotides." She drew a horizontal line between the two strands with her fingertip as Spencer watched. "A genetic marker is a gene or DNA sequence with a known location somewhere on the DNA strand or in a chromosome that is a distinct variation."

"Isn't this stuff really really tiny?"

"Yes."

"Then finding them would be like looking for a needle in a haystack."

"It can seem like it. We need to look at large groups of a population who have the same susceptibility to find the common gene marker, if there is one."

"Computers are your friends."

"Absolutely."

He frowned. "So, not all members of a species have any given marker?"

"No, that's the point. Because sometimes the marker indicates a susceptibility to a particular disease or parasite."

"Are they inherited?"

"Often. Any given marker can also be dominant or recessive, or co-dominant, which complicates things a bit more."

"How does this take you to bees?"

"Well, the European honey bee was the third organism to have its DNA mapped. In 2006, the mapping was completed."

"What were the first two?"

"Fruit flies and mosquitos."

"Those fruit flies again," he teased and she smiled.

"We found out a lot more about bees from their DNA and that mapping."

"Like?"

"Like they have more genes devoted to the sense of smell than to that of taste."

"Makes sense, since they're hunting flower pollen."

"It does. They also have fewer genes governing immunity than the fruit fly or the mosquito, which is interesting and might be a contributing factor to their susceptibility to parasites."

"And the diminishing numbers of bees." Spencer glanced at her glass and Liv took a hint. She had another sip, then he filled it up again. "Are you trying to get me drunk and take advantage of me?" she teased.

"I thought that was your plan for me." He picked up the plates and moved them to the kitchen counter, then put the pitcher of juice and the bottle of prosecco on the coffee table. When Liv stood up, he moved the table away, giving them a clear view of the fire from the couch. She sat down there, leaning back against the leather and felt like purring.

This was decadent.

There was nowhere else she wanted to be.

"You look pleased."

"I'm glad there's nowhere to go and nothing to do."

"I can think of something we can do," Spencer teased. He sat down beside her and stretched out his legs, putting his arm across her shoulder. "Tell me more about the project in England."

"They're trying to discover if there are genetic markers that determine the susceptibility of bees to certain parasites or illnesses."

"To see if there's a genetic reason for something like varroa mites."

"You know something about bees."

"I like bees," he said with a nod, then tapped his tattoo. "They make fruits and vegetables happen."

Liv nodded. "So, we have a list of things that contribute to the death of bees." She ticked them off on her fingers. "Colony collapse disorder, which is when the worker bees suddenly abandon the hive. The American foulbrood, which is a parasite. Varroa mites, another parasite particularly devastating to bees. And tracheal mites."

"More parasites."

"Never mind pesticides and habitat issues and other predators."

"And the goal?"

Liv turned to face him, knowing her excitement showed. "What if we could not only identify the genetic marker that makes bees vulnerable to each of these things, but modify it? What if we could remove it or create an antidote that made bees stronger? What if we could buttress their immunity so they're *less* susceptible?"

Spencer surveyed her, his gaze sliding over her features as surely as a touch. "And it's like a big riddle, or a jigsaw puzzle with ten thousand parts."

"What if I could sort it out, Spencer? What if I could make a difference?"

He raised his hand to her cheek, stroking her skin with his thumb. "Now you're trying to have your way with me," he murmured.

"What?"

"I love when you get excited about your work. It's really sexy."

Liv blushed, but she didn't look away. Spencer's appreciation made her feel sexy, and a lot bolder than she usually was. She took a chance and leaned forward, touching her lips to his. She felt him catch his breath and saw his eyes glitter. "Give me a score on your sexy scale, out of ten," she whispered, daring in her voice

"Eleven," Spencer murmured without hesitation. "I'm yours for the taking."

"I want to see all your tattoos first," Liv said, hearing

that she was a little breathless. "And I want to know why you have them."

"There are only two more."

She reached for the hem of his T-shirt, sliding her hand underneath it so that her palm was against his skin. It felt audacious to seduce him when he wasn't blindfolded, when they were looking into each other's eyes, when there were no secrets about her desire. Liv wanted more and more. "Are you sure?" she asked. "I think I might need to do an inventory..."

He laughed as she tugged off his shirt, then she bent to kiss his nipple, teasing it exactly the way he'd teased hers. He caught his breath. She felt his heart skip a beat. He murmured her name, then his hand landed on the back of her waist. Liv urged him to his back and followed him, wanting to claim all he had to give.

And to give just as much in return.

CHAPTER FIVE

Something had changed.

Spencer saw it in Olivia's eyes, in her posture, he heard it in her tone. Something had softened in her, and brightened. She was demanding as she hadn't been, confident in her touch and her appeal, and he was completely transfixed. The feel of her lips on his nipple, her fingers on his skin, her weight on top of him, made him want to just close his eyes and enjoy.

But he wanted to watch her, too.

He reached up and removed the clip from her hair, letting it spill over her shoulders as she moved to kiss him. He let her take command, and she did with a passion that left him breathless.

And ready.

Her hand slid over his chest to his shoulder. "The compass at the top of your sleeve."

"It points to true north."

"It points to a building that looks a lot like the lodge."

Spencer smiled. "Wolfe Lodge. My true north. The thing that's most important to me."

She kissed the point of the compass. "I guess mine would point to my bee."

"There are bees at the Pines in Honey Hill," Spencer noted.

Olivia smiled, then silenced him with a slow sweet kiss. He eased his hands beneath her shirt, then cupped her breasts in his palms. She squirmed a little, then sat up to discard his sweatshirt. She didn't look like her usual composed self. Her hair was disheveled and her eyes were shining. Her nipples were taut and he caressed them, watching her arch her back in pleasure. She smiled down at him, then tugged at the waistband of his jeans. "I want you naked. Right now."

Spencer grinned and unfastened his jeans. Olivia helped and he was soon lounging on the couch naked as she surveyed him.

"I'll have to remember that recipe," she whispered, then kicked off her own jeans and crawled over him again. She claimed his nipple with a kiss, sucking the peak between her teeth in a move that Spencer knew he'd taught her.

Having her do it to him was enough to make him dizzy. "Is the wolf for your name?" she asked.

On his chest, Spencer had a large tattoo of a wolf with a feather. It was a piece he loved. The feather swirled, the howling wolf silhouetted at its base, a full moon in the middle of the feather, and its tip breaking into a flock of birds that scattered over his skin.

"That and more. As soon as I saw it, I had to have it," he admitted, then Olivia's mouth closed over him and he felt himself shiver. She stroked him, indicating that he should continue. He reached down and let his fingers tangle in her hair, then closed his eyes in rapture.

She was in command and he was content to let her do whatever she wanted, sensing that she needed this change in the balance.

Spencer's voice was husky when he continued.

"The sight of it filled me with wonder, exactly the way I want to feel every day about everything in my life. I want to be in awe. I want to appreciate every bite, every moment, every taste."

He realized that he felt this way with Olivia, that the sight of her filled him with joy, that her smile could change his world, that he wanted to be with her every moment for the duration. He didn't just want her: he loved her.

He gasped as her tongue moved over him, as her teeth grazed him lightly, as she took him almost to the edge, then retreated. "I want to live every day as if it's a new experience." He moaned as she began her assault again, the silk of her hair around his hand. "I want to love with all my heart. I want to give every moment my best. I want to howl at the moon." He caught his breath and his fingers tightened in her hair, because he was close, too close, and he hadn't touched her yet. "Olivia!" he whispered, hearing his own need, and she eased over him. She claimed him with a kiss, a demanding kiss, as if she'd suck him dry. Her passion fed his own and Spencer gripped her waist, wanting to roar when she took him inside her with one smooth move.

"Who's getting lucky now?" she whispered, her eyes filled with mischief and her hair falling all around them.

"Definitely me," he said, smiled up at her. "Let's fix that." He eased his hand between them, inhaling sharply to discover how wet she was, how hard her clitoris was. He watched her sit up and stretch her arms overhead, watched her lips part as he coaxed her to moan. He caressed her as she rode him, their pleasure mounting as they drove each other onward. She looked down at him, desire glittering in the green depths of her eyes, a flush on her cheeks and her breasts.

"Come here," he whispered and she lowered herself

over him, still riding him as her mouth locked over his own. He held her tight and kissed her hungrily, finally rolling her to her back to drive deep inside and make them both roar with satisfaction.

They were breathing heavily when he kissed the corner of her mouth, liking how she smiled. "I love you," he said, holding her gaze, and saw the panic light her own. "Which means I want you to have whatever you want."

She eyed him warily. "Even leave for England?"

"Even that." Spencer heaved a sigh and pushed his hand through her hair. "I'll miss you, and every time I see you, I'll try to convince you to give me another chance, but you have to howl at your moon."

Olivia dropped her gaze. "Isn't there a saying about loving someone enough to let them go?"

"There is. No creature is happy caged."

She brushed her fingertips across his chest piece, her touch lingering on the flock of birds.

"Will you tell me," he dared to ask.

"Tell you what?" Her gaze flicked to his and Spencer knew that she knew exactly what he meant.

"Why you don't believe in something I think is unassailable." He eased her hair back from her cheek and kissed her temple. "Tell me why you don't believe in love, Olivia."

She moved and he rolled to his back, letting her do what she wanted. She braced an elbow on his chest and looked down at him. "It's like what you say about Lexi and doubting she'll come through."

"A learned response."

"Exactly."

He slid his hand up her back, unable to think kindly about anyone breaking her heart. "Tell me about it," he invited, instead of offering to deck some guy.

Olivia nodded slowly. "*Mise en place*," she whispered, then brushed her lips across his. "Let me put all in order then I'll explain."

Spencer was content to wait. They had time. And her agreement to tell him meant that she trusted him.

He knew that trust was the cornerstone of everything.

Could this be the beginning of a future for them?

~

WHERE WOULD SHE START?

Liv felt agitated by even the prospect of confiding in Spencer. Or was she agitated because he'd said those three words—and she'd wanted to respond in kind?

She appreciated that he gave her space and time to think about it. They cleaned up the kitchen together and she helped him organize the perishables in the basement. The basement was bigger and higher than she'd expected. It was made of poured concrete, which must have cost a fortune, and was meticulously clean.

"This is huge," she said without intending to, turning in place and looking around.

"I wanted it done right."

"But it must have cost a fortune."

"It pretty much did."

Liv turned to face Spencer, not wanting to ask the obvious question out loud.

He grinned. "I can guess what you're thinking."

"I thought you put everything into Wolfe Lodge."

"I did, but then something happened." He beckoned to her. "Come on. It's warmer upstairs. I'll tell you there."

She took one last look around the basement, unable to evade the thought that it would make a good lab.

"Once upon a time," Spencer said when they were back in the kitchen. "My great-great-grandfather arrived from England and started to buy land around here."

"The sawmill guy," Liv said, remembering Lexi telling her this story.

"The sawmill guy. He owned a huge chunk of the highlands. Some of it he logged, some of it he sold off, but one piece, the ten acres he thought was the prettiest, he kept pristine. He was working hard and he wasn't married, but he had the idea that one day, he'd build a house on that parcel of land. So, he put away two hundred dollars, saving it for that house."

"When was this?"

"In the late nineteenth century. He never built that house. He married late and kept on working to ensure his kids had a legacy. When he died, his wife invested the money and kept the title to the land. She managed his business and raised his kids, thinking one of them would build the house. But his oldest son moved away to Boston and his second son died in the war. When she died, she left the title and the money, which had grown into a larger sum, to their oldest son, who didn't want to move away from Boston. His oldest son, did move to Bangor to raise his family, but by the time the land and the money came to him, he was well established himself. He put it away for his son."

"Your dad?"

Spencer nodded. "And the same thing happened. By the time this legacy was passed to my dad, he already had the house he wanted in Honey Hill. He tucked it away for me. I didn't know anything about it until Gabriel and I had bought back Wolfe Lodge and re-opened the restaurant. Gabriel had his house in Honey Hill, the one he bought when he sold his restaurant in Portland, but I'd sunk every nickel into the lodge. When my dad found out that I was sleeping in the unrenovated part of the lodge, he gave me the title and the money. He told me to build myself a house that I'd have, regardless of how things went at the lodge. He said he wouldn't give it to me unless I promised to spend the money on building a house and not invest it in the lodge." He raised his gaze to hers. "I thought he was talking about a couple of thousand dollars."

"But he wasn't."

"Compound interest is your friend, especially over a century or so. There was plenty to build this place and to build it exactly the way I wanted it to be. I own it outright, just the way my dad planned, and it's my haven."

"What about Lexi?"

"I'd originally suggested that I could split it with her, but my dad said it was always a legacy for the oldest son. He's not sure Lexi's going to stay in Honey Hill either and it was important to him that this place not ever be sold, the way Wolfe Lodge was." He shook his head. "It really annoyed him that we had to buy it from the guy who let it run into the ground."

"That's a nice legacy."

"It is. And there's a picture of my great-great-grandfather in the lobby of Wolfe Lodge. I wanted to change the name to Hamish Wolfe Lodge, because he was the one who built it in the first place, but Gabriel didn't want to redo all the paperwork and the signage. He also said no one would be able to spell Hamish."

Spencer's smile flashed and Liv knew he didn't really believe that.

She looked around with appreciation, thinking about a family having a presence in one town for over a hundred years. No wonder Spencer thought he belonged here. No wonder he had no plans to leave.

But Liv's roots in Maine weren't nearly that deep.

He was looking out the window. "I think we should seize the moment and bring in some more wood."

The snow was past Liv's knees outside the door and a pile of it cascaded into the cabin when they opened the door. It was still snowing like crazy, the sky filled with swirling white, and the trees were almost buried in the white stuff. It was very quiet outside, just the sound of the wind in their ears as they worked.

"I think you should learn how to make a roast chicken," he said when they were back inside.

"Why?"

"A basic survival skill." He cast her a smile. "Everyone should know how to roast a chicken." Moving with his usual purpose, he chose vegetables from the coolers and began to organize the ingredients on the counter. Liv realized that she was starting to get hungry again and knew she'd be ready for their meal by the time it was done. She helped and enjoyed the rhythm of working with Spencer, even as she planned how she'd answer his question.

❧

THEY WERE WASHING the dishes when Olivia cleared her throat. Spencer glanced her way, but didn't say anything to prompt her. In a way, he wanted this interval to last forever, for the snow to never melt, for him to have the rest of his life to convince her to give them a chance.

In reality, he knew that it was only a matter of time before the power came back on, the snow was plowed, and Olivia went to England.

Could he convince her to come back?

"You wanted to know why I don't believe in love," she said, her voice a little husky.

"Still do."

Her smile was fleeting. "Well, I learned early that while love might exist, it didn't last forever."

"Because nothing is static. You were into science early?" His tone was teasing but she didn't smile.

She shook her head. "It was because of my dad."

Spencer was confused. "Because he died? Did that break your mom's heart?"

"Not exactly, although I would have believed that at the time."

She fell silent again and Spencer gave her a nudge. "Come on. You can't start the story then stop, leaving me in suspense."

"You're right." She frowned. "It's just hard. I haven't talked about it in a long time. Only once, to Brandon."

"So, start at the beginning."

Her gaze dropped to his tattoo and her smile was quick. "Well, he left and Mom said he wasn't coming back, that he'd died."

Spencer felt his eyes narrow. "That sounds like maybe he didn't die."

"Brandon and I never doubted it at the time. Mom said it, so it was true."

"You were little."

"Four. I adored my dad. I thought he could do anything." She sighed. "But then he was gone, and there was just the three of us. I suppose it made a kind of sense that Mom taught us to be independent and self-reliant." She took a deep breath. "She said that as soon as you rely upon someone else, you become vulnerable, and if that person doesn't have your best interests in mind, it will end badly. She taught us to take care of ourselves."

"So, neither of you believe in love."

"It's a fiction, and one that tends to work out particularly badly for women."

"I don't believe that."

"But the problem, Spencer, is that I do. You have to make sure that no one can trash your life on a whim."

Spencer folded his arms across his chest. "What was the whim?"

"My dad didn't die. He left and never came back."

"How do you know?"

"Mom confided in Brandon when he finished high school and he was mad. He went looking for our dad and I never heard the whole story until he came back."

"He found him then."

Olivia nodded. "With his other wife and family, in Nevada. My mom, apparently, was a fling and we were a surprise."

"Hard to have two kids be a surprise."

"And he didn't like the winters and he didn't want to stay, so he left."

"Why did Audrey say he died?"

"I think she was embarrassed, and I think she didn't want to tell us the truth. Honey Hill is a small town. If you're going to lie, it's better if everyone hears the same story."

"Or the truth will come out." Spencer frowned. "But isn't your dad buried at the cemetery?"

"There's an empty box buried under that headstone, apparently. My mom went away for a few days, as if she was collecting his remains, then brought back the box and had the funeral."

"Huh."

"When Brandon came back, she told us the whole story. She said he might as well have died because she knew he wasn't coming back. He took the car and the clothes on his back, and all their money from the bank."

"So, he planned ahead a little bit. The bank can't make that kind of withdrawal late at night."

"Yeah." Olivia nodded. "So, all that stuff in our childhood, of him traveling for work, of him loving us so much, that was all a lie. Apparently, that marriage pre-dated the one with my mom. So the whole thing was a lie because he was a bigamist. An excuse to follow a bio-logical urge." Her lips tightened. "And my mom was hurt, which was why she taught us never to believe in stories of love and happily ever after."

Spencer thought she'd probably taught her kids more than that. It couldn't be an accident that both Brandon and Olivia had been so driven to succeed in school, or that their inclinations had been to excel in math and science respectively.

"You didn't hear from him again? He never came back?" Spencer couldn't believe that any man could forget his kids, especially when one of them was Olivia.

Olivia shook her head. "Not a word, as far as I know. Apparently, the one person she confided in was Jane Watkins."

"If I was going to trust one person in Honey Hill with my secret, it would be Jane."

"And Mom needed her help, too."

"Because your dad took all the money."

Olivia nodded. "They came up with the story of him having a car accident in Pennsylvania. Mom took a trip down there and came home, telling everyone she had his ashes. Jane also lent her the money for the so-called funeral."

"How did she repay Jane?"

"That's how she got into cleaning houses—she started with the Pines, to repay Jane with work instead of money. After the debt was paid, she kept cleaning there. My dad's justification for taking all the money was that he'd earned it. My mom had dropped out of high school to marry him and gotten pregnant with Brandon right away. She'd never had a job, at least until my dad left and she needed one."

"Jane helped," Spencer said, not at all surprised that the older woman had done such a thing, never mind that she'd kept Audrey's secret all these years. "Did you ever talk to him?"

Olivia shook her head. "He didn't care about us," she said, her voice hard. "He was able to just walk away and forget us." She raised her gaze to Spencer's and her eyes were vivid green. "He lied to my mother. He deceived her to get what he wanted and once he had it, he didn't care about the fallout. Her life was hard, harder than it needed to be and harder than she deserved."

"Your mom has a fierce work ethic," Spencer said.

Olivia nodded. "She cleaned houses and took care of us, and took correspondence courses to become a bookkeeper. I don't know when she slept. I look back and am amazed that we were so confident that there'd be enough to eat and that we'd be safe and warm. I remember talking about college and her conviction that both of us would go. We both applied for scholarships to make her proud of us, but she must have been so relieved when we got them."

"You did make her proud."

"And I can't stop doing that now," Olivia said with such ferocity that Spencer understood what drove her. She had her own ambition, but it was amplified by her desire to fulfill her mom's dreams for her.

"That's fair," he said. "Thanks for confiding in me."

She smiled a little and heaved a sigh. "It was easier once I got started. You do understand, don't you?"

"Well, yes and no." Spencer leaned on the counter beside her. "I think there's a flaw in your logic."

"No."

"You can't tell me all this about your mom and her sacrifices for you and Brandon, then insist that love doesn't last."

"That's not romantic love."

"Is it really all that different?"

"I think so. There's no biological urge to make more driving my mom's choices."

"Just the biological need to defend her young."

"Exactly."

"But you're extrapolating from a single example to an entire population. That doesn't seem like a good protocol."

Her expression turned stubborn and Spencer knew he'd found a weak point.

"I mean, my parents are still together and still happy. They still do mushy stuff, so either their love has lasted or they're putting on a good show of it." He held her gaze steadily.

"Or it's mutually beneficial for them to stay together, for financial or social reasons, and they've both committed to their marriage because of that."

Spencer shook his head. "They're in love."

Olivia folded her arms across her chest, her body language telling him that she didn't want to be convinced. "Brandon is just as single as I am, and as our mom is."

"But is it genetic or is it environment?" Spencer whispered. "Are you skeptical because you can't fall in love for the duration, or because your mother taught you to learn from her example."

"I don't think there's any genetic marker for everlasting love."

"But you don't know. Would your results change if you believed?"

"What do you mean?"

"Are people who believe in love more likely to find it and keep it for the duration? Does optimism or conviction or belief influence results?"

Olivia bit her lip. "They definitely influence behavior."

"And maybe that makes all the difference in the world. You know that you perform certain acts better when you believe you can do them, as opposed to when you doubt your abilities. Whenever we try something new, it often doesn't work out as well the first time."

"We need to be confident in the result to achieve it," Olivia mused. "That's interesting."

Spencer wasn't done. "How would your behavior change if you believed in love everlasting."

"We wouldn't be here," Olivia said.

"Really?"

"I would never have made that plan with Lexi if I thought that there was any chance of a relationship. Of course, you'd feel tricked and be annoyed."

"And your choice could have terminated any chance of a future, if it hadn't snowed."

She eyed him. "Because we would have argued and parted."

"Or you would have disappeared with Lexi and not realized that I knew that it was you, and I would be confused as to why you would want me to be unaware of that."

"So, my choice would shape the results of the encounter."

Spencer lifted a hand. It seemed self-evident to him. He watched Olivia think it through.

"Whereas if I had thought there might be a relationship, I could have asked you out."

"Or just given me a hint of your feelings," Spencer

said. "I would have jumped at the chance to try to convince you to give me a try."

"Really?" She looked very pleased by that.

"Absolutely."

"But you always treated me like another little sister."

"Because you always acted like I was another big brother. I didn't want to do anything that meant I might not see you at all."

Olivia's smile turned mischievous and her voice dropped low. "And what would you have done, if you'd had a little encouragement from me?"

"Oh, something like this," he murmured, bending to brush his lips across hers.

"That wouldn't have convinced me," she said and he grinned.

"Something like this," he said, kissing her ear and drawing her into his arms.

"Better, but I still wouldn't have been sold."

"Something like this," he whispered before capturing her lips with his own. She made a little purr of satisfaction, a sound that got him right where he lived, and leaned against him. Spencer deepened his kiss, lifting her against him, guessing that this was his another chance to make his argument. He bent and scooped her up in his arms, then carried her to the bedroom, glad he knew the obstacles well enough that he didn't have to break his kiss.

He didn't know how long it would be before they were compelled to rejoin the real world, but he was going to make every moment count.

≈

IT HAD to be very early in the morning when Olivia heard a click and a whirr. She opened her eyes and sat up, well aware of the weight of Spencer's arm around her waist. She realized she'd heard the sound of the fridge starting.

And there was a light in the bathroom again.

She glanced down to find Spencer watching her. He looked warm and relaxed, his hair tousled, and so attractive that her heart clenched. They'd had sex so many times, but it just got better.

It had changed from having sex to making love.

It couldn't last, even if it felt like it might. Liv refused to be fooled.

She was afraid of making a promise that she might not be able to keep. She knew what she wanted to say, but the last thing she wanted to do was to end up lying to this man, even if the words were well-intentioned when they passed her lips. Panic rose within her and her heart skipped a beat, but his gaze never wavered from her own.

He lifted his other hand and beckoned to her. "Again," he murmured, his voice a low growl that she couldn't resist. "While the hot water heats."

Liv eased back into his embrace and loved how his arms closed around her. They loved sweetly and slowly, eyes wide open, so attuned to each other's likes and needs that Liv was shaken by the power of their union.

When Spencer left the bed, she pretended to be dozing, so she could think. It couldn't continue to get better, to be more potent, to be more compelling. This had to be the end point, or close to it. During these days, she'd felt cherished by him, and if life could be like this forever, she would sign up in a minute.

But nothing lasted forever. Liv knew that in her very bones.

She compelled herself to think of her dad.

She thought of her mom, who hadn't realized that Olivia had heard her weeping.

And she acknowledged that she didn't have it in her to surrender that power over her own happiness to anyone.

Even to Spencer, who was the most trustworthy and thoughtful man she'd ever known. It wasn't his fault. It was just biology.

Liv didn't want to live her life in fear of being hurt or being left. She didn't want to be waiting for the bad news, because that would keep her from enjoying what was good. It wouldn't be fair to Spencer, who savored every moment and every experience.

And so, she had to go.

She heard the sounds of a vehicle and knew the end had come.

Leaving was the right thing to do, even though it felt so very wrong.

It would be kinder in the long run, even though it was painful in the moment. Spencer would fall in love with someone who could meet him halfway and return his trust.

Liv was never going to come back to Honey Hill to see that.

~

SPENCER HAD SUSPECTED the truth when the power came back on, but he knew it for certain the moment that Olivia came into the kitchen. She spared him a smile that didn't reach her eyes when she accepted the coffee from him. She closed her eyes when she took a sip and he took some satisfaction in that. "It's so good. Thank you."

Even her tone was dismissive.

He'd lost.

He didn't have to like it.

He'd plugged in both of their phones and she picked up hers, turning it on and watching the messages flow.

"Did they rebook your flight?" he asked, trying to keep the frustration from his voice.

Olivia nodded. "Tonight. I'll just have time to visit my mom." She winced then. "The guy who was buying Mindy bought another car instead."

"Leave Mindy with me."

She raised her gaze to his. "I'm not coming back, Spencer."

He nodded understanding. "Then sell her to me."

"You don't need another vehicle. You have a truck..."

"A pick-up. I've been thinking about getting something more passenger-friendly. It's a solution that would work for both of us."

She was reluctant to even have that much of a tie between them and Spencer saw it immediately.

He forced a smile. "Who else is going to let Mindy keep her name?"

"If you're sure..."

"I am. What was he going to pay you? I'll come around to your mom's with the money this afternoon. Or I could drive you to the airport."

Olivia looked concerned.

"Just friends," Spencer said. "I know that's what you want."

Her smile was tentative. "That's a lot of driving for you."

He shrugged, knowing he'd be glad of every second in her presence. "I don't mind. Your mom could come, too, and see you off."

Their gazes held one last time. Spencer's mouth was dry and he felt as if he was filled with words and arguments in his own favor. But he'd tried, and she wasn't convinced. As much as he wished otherwise, he respected her right to choose.

Even if she didn't choose him.

Steps sounded on the porch and there was a flurry of knocking at the door. He turned away and opened the door to Lexi, who fell into the cabin with a ton of snow. "Hey, you two!" she said, her eyes alight with the expectation that something had happened. "How's that magic tattoo, Liv?"

Olivia put down her mug and reached for her jacket. "I told you there was no such thing as magic, Lexi." She flicked a glance at Spencer. "Sometimes you have to run an experiment to be sure," she added softly as if Spencer needed any more confirmation that he'd lost.

CHAPTER SIX

The ride to the airport was quiet. Liv drove Mindy, knowing it would be the last time, and her mom sat beside her. Spencer was in the back, and even though he didn't say much, Liv was keenly aware of his presence.

Of his hope.

Of the fact that she couldn't fulfill it.

When they got to the airport, he was gruff. "I'll watch the car. Go to the gate with her, Audrey. You don't know when you'll see each other again."

Liv got out and Spencer moved to get into the driver's seat. He gave her an intent look but didn't touch her, his eyes so blue that the sight stole her breath away. "Have a good flight," he said softly, his gaze sliding over her. "You know where to find me."

Liv's mouth was dry and her throat was tight. She felt her tears well as she nodded, and she wished in that moment that she could believe, even for a little bit of time, just because she wasn't ready for this to end. She caught at his sleeve and kissed his cheek quickly. He'd shaved and she felt how smooth his skin was in contrast to their few days of seclusion, and smelled his cologne. She was keenly aware of his warmth in a way that was new, that she'd like to explore even more, and she felt that tingle of desire that seemed to only get stronger in his presence.

It was better, she told herself, to walk away now, when everything was at its peak. She couldn't bear the possibility of watching this incredible feeling fade to nothing before her eyes. She couldn't stand if it she was the one who broke his heart or hurt him in any way.

"Thank you," she said, and his gaze clung to hers for a long moment.

Someone honked behind them and he nodded once, then got into the car. Adjusting the seat seemed to take all of his attention. Her mom was standing on the curb with Liv's suitcase and she joined her, linking arms to walk into the terminal.

Liv didn't look back.

Her mom didn't comment on Spencer. They talked about everything and nothing, then hugged tightly before Liv went through security. "I'll call you when I get there."

Audrey pushed her hands into her pockets and nodded, clearly blinking back tears. "I'm so proud of you, Livvie. Never forget that."

"I love you, Mom."

She knew they weren't parting forever. Her mom had already talked about making a visit to England during the summer. But Liv felt as if she had been hollowed out, scraped raw, left alone. Was this the downside of being mindful? Would every sensation be more powerful? In a way, the ache of parting made her want to go back, to be numb again, but then she thought of Spencer's touch and couldn't regret a thing.

Her feelings would fade. She'd lose herself in her work again. She was independent and logical and confronted with an excellent challenge.

She was going to make a difference to the bees.

~

JUST LIKE THAT, Olivia was gone.

With no apparent plans to come back to Honey Hill anytime soon.

Spencer didn't like it.

But there wasn't a lot he could do about it. The way he saw it, he'd argued his side as well as he could given the time constraints. Whatever would be would be.

And if he was a bit grumpy in the kitchen at the lodge in the upcoming weeks or months, he figured Gabriel had it coming.

He sat in the car at the airport and waited for Audrey.

The problem was that he'd seen the yearning in Olivia's eyes when he'd made his confession. On some level, she either believed in love or wanted to—she just didn't think it was for her.

That was a helluva legacy for her father to leave.

He was feeling irritable when Audrey returned to the car, but he tried to hide it. It wasn't her fault and they had a long drive ahead of them. He opened her door for her and forced a smile.

"Nice of you to buy Mindy," she said, her tone neutral.

"I felt bad that Olivia lost her buyer because of the snow."

"That's pretty generous," Audrey noted.

Spencer shrugged and pulled into the traffic. "I've been thinking about getting rid of the truck. I'll give this a try and can always sell if it doesn't work out."

Audrey nodded understanding. She was a slender woman with dark hair that she wore short. She did the bookkeeping at the lodge and seldom volunteered more than was absolutely necessary. She was polite, but not a warm person. Spencer thought of her as all angles and efficiency.

"I thought there might have been another reason," she said after they'd been silent for a long while.

"Like what?"

Audrey shrugged. "It was just a thought. There seemed to be a little tension today, and I didn't realize you knew each other well enough for that."

Spencer was well aware that Lexi had told Audrey that Olivia had stayed with her, and he wasn't going to be the one who revealed the truth. "Well, we both know Lexi."

Audrey made a non-committal sound. "I think Livvie will enjoy that work in England."

"Yes. I believe she will."

They drove in silence again. The roads were good, having been plowed and salted, but there wasn't much traffic. They were making good time.

Spencer realized he had an opportunity to learn more about Olivia from the person who knew her best. He took a deep breath. "She told me about her dad."

He felt Audrey turn to look at him in her surprise. "Why would she do that?"

"Because I told her that I love her. I think she might love me, but she's afraid to give us a chance. She says there's no such thing as love, that attraction is a biological impulse to encourage us to mate."

"Ah," Audrey said and glanced out the window. She frowned. "Jeremy's legacy."

"Or yours?" he dared to ask.

Audrey didn't take offense. "You're right. Neither she nor Brandon are romantics, and I admit that I made sure of that."

"I'd like to try to change her mind."

"Are you trying to impose your objectives on her?" Audrey shook her head. "I don't like that much, Spencer."

"No. I'd like her to give us a chance. I'll stand by her choice. I just want to know why she's not even interested in trying."

"Didn't she make her choice by going to England?" Audrey asked quietly and Spencer sighed.

He frowned, nodded, and shut up.

They continued in silence until Audrey sighed. "I understand why you might love her, Spencer. I love her with all my heart."

"Then why teach her to close herself to love? Won't it hold her back from happiness?"

"I thought it would guarantee her happiness, if she found it in herself instead of relying upon a man to provide it." Audrey shook her head and sighed. "She was only four, Spencer. She was devastated by Jeremy's departure. He was everything to her. Because I saw her hurt so badly, I never ever wanted her to go through it again. I tried to protect her from heartbreak."

Spencer nodded, recalling his own reaction when he'd thought that some other guy had broken Olivia's heart. "I understand."

Again, silence filled the car, until Spencer pulled into Audrey's driveway. She hesitated before getting out of the car. "Did you tell her how you feel?"

Spencer nodded.

Audrey frowned. "She didn't want to go." She turned to face him, her gaze softer than it had been. "I couldn't figure out why, but maybe now we both know."

"Maybe it doesn't matter."

"Maybe it will." She smiled and touched his hand

again. "Thank you for driving me to the airport to see Livvie on her way, Spencer."

"You're welcome. Thanks for confiding in me."

"Good luck," she said softly before she got out of the car.

Spencer had a feeling he was going to need all the luck he could get.

~

LIV COULDN'T BELIEVE the power of her short time with Spencer. In just a couple of days, he'd changed her perspective completely and that had turned her life upside-down. She went through all the motions and she doubted that anyone realized the turmoil of her thoughts.

Attraction was supposed to be fleeting. It was intended to drive people to make and make more. Pure biology. Once lust was satisfied, desire should vanish.

Not get stronger.

Once the object of desire was out of view, lust should fade. Thoughts should wander. The eye should seek another object of desire.

But Spencer showed no inclination to fade from Liv's thoughts and her desire for him—and his company —was stronger than ever.

She was sure she just had to wait it out.

But every day proved her wrong.

She missed him so much that she ached with it.

She joined the team in Cambridge and found them to be professional and enthused. She reviewed the work that had been done and the plans for the future, and accepted her share of the workload. There was some discussion about a need to expand the sample and look at bees in other geographic regions as a future endeavor.

The lab was perfectly organized, in Liv's view, and she had been known to change things around to make them more logical. There were no changes she could suggest.

The flat they'd arranged for her was compact and ideally located. She could walk everywhere she needed to go, which was great. Her coworkers were excellent and she could see already that she'd be contributing to a meaningful endeavor.

It was exactly what she'd wanted and what she'd expected.

But it disappointed her in an unexpected way—because Liv herself was different.

She tasted her food more than she had before, and she felt sensation more keenly than she had just a week before. She found pleasure in the softness of a knit collar under her chin, the smoothness of the cotton sheets on her bed, the weight of a wool blanket on a cool night. She smelled the lanolin in the wool and the coffee made in the morning by her neighbor. She examined the oranges at the market, recalling Spencer's advice, and was ridiculously pleased when she picked three in row that were thin-skinned and juicy.

She thought of him at the strangest times: when she was alone at night, of course, but also during the daytime. The memory of his smile would pop into her thoughts while she was at the lab and she would smile herself. She heard someone laugh at the pub, when she went out for a pint with her coworkers on her first Friday night, and her heart skipped with the certainty that it was him. It wasn't and the power of her disappointment surprised her.

Maybe absence really did make the heart grow fonder.

Maybe what she felt for Spencer was more than attraction or lust.

Could it be that Spencer's hypothesis was right and not her own?

Two weeks after her arrival, Liv paused at the grocery to consider a small chicken in the poultry display. She'd returned to her old habit of eating things from cans and prepared foods, but she found the food unsatisfying as she never had before. She eyed the chicken and her mouth watered. It was easy to recall the chicken Spencer had roasted and how delicious it had been, and to be tempted...

Liv forced herself to be rational. It would be too much meat for one person. It wouldn't taste nearly as good because she couldn't cook as well as Spencer. It had been the company that had made the meal.

She missed him.

And Liv didn't know what to do about that. It was new for her. Different. Unwelcome. Maybe it was even rational.

Did she love Spencer?

Just the thought made her heart clench.

Liv found herself hoping her mom would share some news of Spencer during their regular calls, but Audrey never even mentioned him.

Finally, she asked.

"Grumpy as a bear," her mom supplied. "I'm avoiding him." She paused for a moment. "Have you talked to him?"

"Of course not."

Her mother made a skeptical sound, although Liv didn't know whether she doubted that Liv hadn't talked to Spencer, or was expressing an opinion of her decision not to do so.

Liv changed the subject. "How are Jane's bees?"

Her mother sighed. "Not good."

That made no sense. It was May. The hives should be humming with activity again. "What do you mean?"

"When Jane did her spring check of the hives, there were a lot of dead bees. She's devastated..."

"Mom," Liv interrupted her mom. "We need to find out what killed them. If it's a parasite, the survivors could be spreading it to each other."

"Well, how will we do that?"

"Jane would have to preserve them. Let me pull out my notes..."

"Preserve them for who, Livvie?" her mom asked, ever practical. "Jane doesn't need a lot of dead bees around, whether they're preserved or not."

"I have an idea," Liv confessed, feeling that rush of audacity again, the one that was becoming more familiar. She liked it now. It made her feel powerful. "Could you give me Jane's number, please, and I'll explain as soon as I can."

~

IT WAS A COLD SPRING, one that never seemed inclined to get started. Spencer could relate to that. He was thinking that hibernation was under-rated.

It would be warmer for a day, just enough for a few inches of snow to melt, then it would snow again. Finally, the thaw came, but the skies were overcast and it seemed to Spencer that everything was grey and without hope. Then they had rain in Honey Hill, rain so cold and driving that Spencer thought the ground would never be dry again.

Work progressed on the lodge and the summer bookings began to add up. There was a little bit of fresh produce coming in—the first of the asparagus and rhubarb, both from greenhouses to the south. He was trying to get excited about possibilities and failing completely.

Mostly, he was thinking about Olivia.

His phone rang one Tuesday afternoon almost exactly three weeks after she'd left—although he told himself he wasn't counting the days. Spencer was waiting on an artisan cheesemaker who always seemed to be late. He didn't recognize the number, so he answered, expecting it to be the cheesemaker using someone else's phone.

"Spencer Wolfe."

The line had an echo on it, like the echo of a satellite.

Like a long distance call.

He straightened.

"Spencer? Is that you?"

It was Olivia, sounding as if she was at the bottom of the ocean, or at least that far away.

"Olivia! Hi." He couldn't keep the pleasure from his voice and realized belatedly that he sounded like a lovesick kid. He felt the back of his neck heat and ran a hand over it, embarrassed by his enthusiasm.

"I always liked that you called me by my full name," she said, surprising him with the words.

"Why?"

"I don't know. It seemed special."

Spencer bit back the urge to insist that she was special. "It's a pretty name. I like it better than Liv or Livvie."

"So do I." Her voice dropped. "When *you* say it."

Spencer folded his arms across his chest, not wanting to get his hopes up. "How's England? And the research project?"

"Good. Great, really. Fascinating work and a fabulous team. I'm learning a lot and I feel like I'm making a difference."

"Great." Surely she hadn't called to tell him she was never ever coming back?

"How's Mindy?"

"Running perfectly."

Neither of them said anything for a moment but even the silence seemed to echo.

"Look," Olivia said, her words coming in a rush. "I wanted to try to cook something."

"Good for you."

"But you only taught me recipes for things that are supposed to lead to sex, and there's no one I want to get lucky with."

"No one?"

She cleared her throat a little and he could imagine that she was blushing a bit. "No one in close proximity."

"So, you're scared to cook in case results aren't desirable," Spencer guessed.

"I want to roast a chicken," she said, sounding determined. "I want to roast a chicken and I want to make love on the kitchen counter while it's cooking, when the whole apartment smells delicious, and I want to learn how to make it taste even better, and I want to keep making love all night long." She caught her breath. "It would be kind of like howling at the moon or proving I'm alive or showing someone how I feel. It's something I've never done before and ever since I thought of it, I can't stop thinking about it."

"And so you called me for the recipe?" Spencer prompted, because she sounded nervous and he wanted her to smile.

She almost laughed, then her next words were serious. "I called to see if you had any interest in being in closer proximity."

Spencer stilled. He knew he hadn't misunderstood her.

Olivia cleared her throat then spoke in a rush. "Because I can't stop thinking about you, either, which makes me think that your hypothesis was the right one."

Everything in Spencer was tight. "You want to find out?"

"I think this calls for a very long and very intimate experiment," she whispered. "It could take years. Maybe decades." He heard her swallow. "If you're interested."

"Give me your address," he replied softly.

She did then continued with the same haste. "I'd go shopping but I don't know how to pick a good chicken."

"I'll do it."

"Okay."

He heard her smile then and began to smile himself. "Okay."

"Come soon."

"Absolutely."

There was no chance that Spencer would miss the very next flight.

෴

LIV COULDN'T BELIEVE she'd done it.

She'd called Spencer.

She'd asked him to come.

She'd been within a whisker of telling him the truth and had only stopped because she wanted to see his eyes when she made her confession.

She didn't sleep that night, or only just barely. She knew the flights from the east coast arrived at Heathrow early in the morning. She showered and dressed and cleaned her flat one last time, suspecting that he'd arrive around nine. She used her new grinder and made a pot of coffee.

It was good, but she obviously needed more instruction.

She was standing at the main window, the one with the view of the street, with her hands wrapped around her mug when a familiar figure got out of a taxi. Spencer stood and looked around, orienting himself. He had only a small backpack, as if he'd grabbed essentials and hurried to the airport.

As if he was as ready to see her as she was to see him.

Liv knocked on the glass and waved, waiting until he looked up. Then she grabbed her keys and ran down the stairs, erupting into the street. He caught her up and kissed her, swinging her around—much to the amusement of the other pedestrians.

"I made coffee," she confessed.

"I love you," he replied, as if that truth was obvious and would never change. That gave Olivia the confidence to tease him a little.

"Because I made coffee?" She felt light and happy, just because he was with her, just because he was looking at her as if she was the amazing one.

"Because you are who you are. Because you learn and try new things." He stole a quick kiss and his next words were husky. "Because you called and told me what you wanted."

"That's not all I wanted to tell you." Liv smiled when his gaze brightened. "I love you, too. I wanted to tell you in person."

The confession didn't hurt at all. She felt better having said it and knew it was the truth.

"Fair enough." Spencer smiled with lazy satisfaction. He set her on her feet, keeping her in the circle of his arms. "The question is: if we cook a roast chicken together, which one of us will be getting lucky?" He kissed her before she could laugh or reply.

Liv flung her arms around his neck, kissing him back so that he didn't doubt his welcome.

"I missed you, Olivia," he whispered against her throat and she closed her eyes against the surge of pleasure she felt in hearing him say her name.

"I missed you so much," she admitted, and his arms tightened around her even as he pulled back to look into her eyes.

"And I'm so glad you want to cook with *me*."

"Only you."

"Works for me."

Liv grabbed his hand and tugged him toward the door to her flat. "It's tiny," she warned him as they climbed the stairs. She urged him into the space and he had to duck his head a bit to avoid hitting it on a beam. He looked really tall in the small space, but he scanned it and nodded. "But I won't be here much longer."

He glanced her way in surprise. "Why's that?"

Liv clasped her hands together, knowing that once she started to tell him, the words would tumble out. "We had a discussion in the lab about refining our results because we're not narrowing in on a solution very quickly. I suggested that we could compare genetic markers found in different species of bees, because they all seem to have susceptibility to certain parasites." Spencer was very still, his eyes that bright blue that made her heart skip. "So, I called Jane at the Pines and asked if I could use some of her dead bees for research."

"She found a lot of dead ones in the hive this spring," Spencer said with care.

"I know. My mom told me. And I saw an opportunity, so I called Jane and she agreed, because she wants to know how to help her bees."

"Is it legal to ship bees internationally?"

"It's not advisable if they've died of disease." Liv took a deep breath. "I gave her instructions on preserving them, and they're waiting for me in Honey Hill. We've got some leads on funding for equipment. All I need is lab space."

"In Bangor?"

Liv shook her head. "I was thinking in Honey Hill because I'd like to continue with my cooking lessons, too." She smiled. "You spoiled me, Spencer. I want it all now."

Spencer smiled slowly and closed the distance between them. He raised a hand to her chin, sliding his fingers across her skin in a slow caress that melted her knees. "Are you coming home with me?"

"If you can stay a week to wait for me."

"Deal." He bent and kissed her lightly, looked into her eyes, then slanted his mouth to claim her lips. He deepened his kiss and lifted her to her toes, crushing her against his chest, and Liv closed her eyes.

His kiss got better every time.

"What changed your mind?" he murmured when she gave him a chance.

"You did. You convinced me that I needed to howl at the moon."

Spencer grinned, then kissed her again, scooping her up and heading for her narrow bed. Liv didn't care how crowded it was. She'd be with him again and she couldn't wait.

This was the beginning of a new and exciting experiment, one that Liv thought might very well last all of her life.

And she was just fine with that.

~

IT WAS a sunny afternoon in the middle of May when Chynna finally arrived at Flatiron Five. She'd taken her time walking uptown from Chinatown, admiring the cut flowers for sale, the sight of people without their heavy coats, the laughter from the first brave souls to sit on outdoor patios. The outdoor market on Fifth Ave. was bustling with new vendors and she browsed before going into the shop to work.

Tristan was on the front desk, bobbing his head. He had a tarot card under one claw and gave her a bright look when she stepped into the shop.

Chynna glanced up to her bulletin board, where she'd tucked the three cards chosen for Liv's tattoo. The third one had been plucked from the board.

"Is it done?" she asked the bird and he cawed with enthusiasm.

Chynna smiled as she eased the card from beneath his weight. She turned it over so that she could see the illustration on the face of The Lovers, then gave Tristan a treat and slid all three cards back into her tarot deck. There were still a few days to the next full moon, but they—Chynna, Tristan, and the tarot cards—were ready.

~

JUST ONE VACATION NIGHT
FLATIRON FIVE TATTOO #2

Reyna knows happily-ever-after isn't in her future...

But after three years of solitude, Reyna is ready for a fling. She's learned her lesson with bad boys and long-term expectations, so her neighbor's visiting nephew is the perfect man to lead into temptation. But Kade has a gift for breaking her rules and ensuring Reyna doesn't regret it, which means one night becomes two...

Kade believes in putting the past where it belongs...

Kade was always waiting for the right woman, and one night with Reyna convinces him that he's found her. It's more than great sex and good conversation: Reyna's determination to shape her life inspires him to rebuild his own, and he knows they'll be a great team. All he has to do is convince her to take a chance on him and forever. When Reyna's past catches up to them both, will it destroy their new partnership before the future begins?

~

Honey Hill—May 15

The little heart on Reyna's butterfly tattoo burned.

It felt like it was on fire, which was bizarre because the rest of the tattoo didn't hurt at all. It had healed beautifully, all of it, but Reyna could feel that little heart.

All the time.

It almost pulsed.

It wasn't painful, just always present. A reminder. It made her think about her conversation with Chynna and mull on it more than she would have otherwise. It made her think about her wish not to be alone anymore, the one she never thought would come true.

Even more odd, the heart had heated up a notch when she'd heard that Olivia had called Spencer from England and that he'd flown there the same day. The story in town was that they were coming back to Honey Hill together, as a couple.

Had Chynna's tattoo worked for Olivia?

Even if it hadn't, even if Reyna discarded the whole situation and its resolution as coincidence, there was still this insistent warmth on the back of her shoulders.

It made her think about possibilities.

It made her remember things she wanted to forget or at least never experience again. Once was enough for some events.

But despite her painful memories, Reyna found herself yearning for the feel of a man's hands on her skin. She didn't miss being in a relationship, the expectations and the compromises, and all the drama. She missed sex, though. Slow, thorough sex. There really wasn't a good substitute for a gorgeous man determined to please. Just the thought made her yearn a little more. She'd been as chaste as a nun for three years and this spring, the status quo wasn't nearly good enough. She was impatient. Ready for a caress. More than ready to take a chance.

If this was spring fever, Reyna knew how to get rid of it.

One man.

One night.

Multiple mind-blowing orgasms.

It sounded like a great plan and a simple formula, but there was one considerable snag. There were many things Reyna loved about living in the town of Honey Hill, but the very low number of eligible men wasn't one of them. Initially, she'd felt safer with so few men her age in the vicinity, but as her confidence had returned, she'd begun to see the situation as less than ideal.

If Reyna ignored the guys she didn't think were attractive, the ones who were too old or too young, the ones she'd heard strange stories about, and the ones she knew weren't interested in her, the list of candidates became very, very small.

In fact, there was just one potential recipient of her affections.

Kade Sullivan.

Reyna knew she wasn't the only one who had noticed the arrival of one very eligible, very hot male in Honey Hill. The nephew of the retired couple who lived across the street from Reyna, Kade was obviously close to his aunt and uncle. He'd come to stay, apparently to help them with some maintenance on their home. He was maybe a couple of years older than Reyna, trim and muscular. Reyna had appreciated the view of him on their roof when he'd checked the chimneys, his tall figure silhouetted against the sky. He walked the main street of Honey Hill at regular intervals, from one end of the block to the other, as he made his way to the general store for supplies. Reyna was at the window of her shop each and every time he passed by. She just couldn't resist a look.

How long was he staying?

Where did he usually live?

Speculation was rife, but Reyna wasn't sure of the truth. The Sullivans were too busy enjoying his company to talk to their neighbors about him. Reyna knew only that he was gorgeous, apparently single, and that time was of the essence.

Who knew how long he'd stay?

He must be a contractor or a carpenter, helping out his aunt and uncle on his vacation or between jobs. Reyna liked him for that alone.

Never mind the novelty of a nice guy.

Kade was obviously a straight arrow. Level gaze, short hair, he was as far from Reyna's typical choice of a bad boy with a reputation as could be. He'd been clean-shaven when he arrived, but now had about three days' growth of beard. He must have been trimming it because it didn't get longer—it didn't make him look disreputable either. He was polite to old ladies, even nosy Mrs. Foster. He'd helped Mitch Gardener's son launch his kite, over and over again, the previous Saturday. He seemed to have endless patience with his aunt and uncle's home, another Victorian much like Reyna's own. She knew how much trouble those old houses could be.

Maybe instead taking a risk with a bad boy, it was time for Reyna to ask for what she wanted—instead of taking what a man offered.

The butterfly seemed to hum in agreement.

Reyna was going to lead Kade Sullivan astray, for just one night.

She wouldn't regret it, and she'd make sure he didn't either.

∼

Just One Vacation Night
Flatiron Five Tattoo #2
Available Now!

∼

ABOUT THE AUTHOR

Deborah Cooke sold her first book in 1992, a medieval romance called **Romance of the Rose** published under her pseudonym Claire Delacroix. Since then, she has published over fifty novels in a wide variety of sub-genres, including historical romance, contemporary romance, paranormal romance, fantasy romance, time-travel romance, women's fiction, paranormal young adult and fantasy with romantic elements. She has published under the names Claire Delacroix, Claire Cross and Deborah Cooke. **The Beauty**, part of her successful Bride Quest series of historical romances, was her first title to land on the *New York Times* List of Bestselling Books. Her books routinely appear on other bestseller lists and have won numerous awards. In 2009, she was the writer-in-residence at the Toronto Public Library, the first time the library has hosted a residency focused on the romance genre. In 2012, she was honored to receive the Romance Writers of America's Mentor of the Year Award.

Currently, she writes contemporary romances and paranormal romances under the name Deborah Cooke. She also writes medieval romances as Claire Delacroix. Deborah lives in Canada with her husband and family, as well as far too many unfinished knitting projects.

Http://DeborahCooke.com

Printed in Great Britain
by Amazon